# NOSFERATU

# NOSFERATU

A NOVEL

## Jim Shepard

ALFRED A. KNOPF   NEW YORK   1998

THIS IS A BORZOI BOOK
PUBLISHED BY ALFRED A. KNOPF, INC.

www.randomhouse.com

Portions of this novel previously appeared in *TriQuarterly,* the
*Southwest Review,* the *Michigan Quarterly Review,* and *DoubleTake.*

Library of Congress Cataloging-in-Publication Data
Shepard, Jim.
Nosferatu : a novel / Jim Shepard. — 1st ed.
p.   cm.
ISBN 0-679-44667-2 (alk. paper)
1. Murnau, F. W. (Friedrich Wilhelm), 1889–1931—Fiction.
2. Motion picture producers and directors—Germany—Fiction.
3. Nosferatu (Motion picture)—Fiction. I. Title.
PS3569.H39384N67    1997
813'.54—dc21         97-34371
CIP

Manufactured in the United States of America

First Edition

*For Karen*

# CHARLOTTENBURG,
# 1907

HE FIRST noted sleeplessness in his journal in May of 1907. That year he turned eighteen, passed his *Abitur* in Kassel, and moved to Berlin-Charlottenburg to study philology. There he got to know Hans Ehrenbaum-Degele, who was first a schoolmate and then a soulmate. Their friendship made a poet out of Ehrenbaum-Degele, and a filmmaker out of Murnau.

Murnau was still at that point named Friedrich Wilhelm Plumpe. He was a boy from the provinces. His friend's mother was a well-known opera singer, and the father a wealthy banker. They lived in an oversized villa in the Grunewald. The family was passionately interested in culture, which was a sea change from what Wilhelm was used to at home.

Two years later, under the cover of darkness, he and his friend would travel south to an inn in the Upper Bavarian town of Murnau, where the next morning, in a sober, private ceremony, the student Wilhelm Plumpe would give up his cloddish surname and take the name with which he would become renowned.

But that August morning in 1907 he left his home with only his mother to part from. He was sick from nervous anticipation. He continually annoyed and comforted himself by rubbing his thumb over his fist. His mother told him to try to make friends at school. Begin over. And not to get the reputation of being quiet. Well-intended advice, but when the stars sang to the moon, he thought, then he'd be talkative and likeable.

His father's only remark as he prepared to go was "A black tie? Has there been the death of a stage actor?"

His two older brothers, already resentful of the fuss and their mother's agitation, declined to come down to see him off.

He rode the train east in a first-class compartment. His father had absolutely ruled out such an indulgence, and his mother had slipped him the extra money to change the fare. For most of the trip he rode under the insolent scrutiny of two immaculately dressed young men across the aisle. One featured a silk collar with an iridescent rose-and-copper tie, and spar-rock cuff links. Wilhelm was wearing his only suit. On either side of him were trunks too large for the baggage racks: the farmboy, in from the country with all his worldly possessions.

He managed his first hellos as a man of the world. The two young men responded with the thin smiles they might offer the mother of a harelipped infant. Wilhelm gave their expressions the benefit of the doubt and spent the rest of the trip empty-headed with self-conscious excitement. From time to time he peered through his windowpane at the sodden countryside, and through that wet glass he first viewed Berlin's landscape of moraines.

His grand entrance to Charlottenburg involved having to wrestle his trunks off the passenger step of the lounge car. The immaculate fellow passengers had long since left. One trunk became wedged. He heard titters behind him. He sweated and pulled. His embarrassment increased. He felt he should have been wearing a straw hat and carrying chickens in a cage.

Hans Ehrenbaum-Degele was across the platform, watching from a bench. He looked comfortably situated. His compact valise sat parallel to his feet.

For Wilhelm it was as if he'd caught his first glimpse of life's splendor, which in its fullness had always surrounded him, veiled from view and far off. He stared while extricating his trunks. The boy at whom he stared was finely freckled. He had a pleasant squint. He had shell-blue eyes, and the tolerant expression of someone watching a small animal attempt something inexplicable.

Behind Wilhelm an elderly woman finally asked if he needed

assistance. Wilhelm forgot to speak, for looking at the boy on the bench.

Later he asked his new friend why he hadn't helped.

Hans said he thought it was something he should manage by himself—first day and all that. He then asked why, if he had seemed so rude, Wilhelm had come over and introduced himself.

All this had transpired while they shared a hansom to school. Wilhelm, emboldened by his first day of adventure, had confided that he'd thought to himself, If you don't talk to him now, you'll only waste weeks trying to find him again. And so he had stacked his two trunks and lumbered over, teetering under the weight.

At a pub outside of the school grounds, his new friend asked the hansom to stop and wait. Inside, he bought them each a tumbler of milk. He seemed as unembarrassed in a foreign place as an Englishman.

He was barrel-chested. His cheekbones were broad, and the unlined quality of his face reminded Wilhelm of bread dough. His lower lip was prominent, as if he were undecided between deep thought and a tantrum.

He chatted about opera and the theater. Wilhelm felt as though they were picking up the thread of a conversation they'd already begun.

He watched his new friend surreptitiously. He could make out the shadow of his eyelashes. He watched him drink his milk. Within a half hour, he was trying to transmit looks in which he'd invested his heart and soul. Hans carried on with his conversation unfazed.

Hans Ehrenbaum-Degele wanted to know what the new arrival's goals were in life. Intimidated, Wilhelm said, "The theater." He had never vocalized that ambition before. He'd told his parents he intended to study philology.

He lapsed into embarrassed silence.

Hans volunteered that besides poetry, he had no specific

dreams; he was still in the "unencumbered good time" of his youth. He turned his foot inward every so often in order to glance at his shoes, which evidently pleased him.

For the rest of the ride he held forth in a mini-lecture. They might be studying philology, he said, but their ultimate concern was art, which meant they should consider themselves artists. Berlin was open to innovation. The Secessionists had triumphed over the academicians; the galleries were supportive; the press willing to review new directions. Berliners were open-minded, difficult to please, skeptical and critical. In a nutshell, the city was an express, hurtling forward.

Periodically, Wilhelm nodded feebly.

Expressionism, for example, had originated in the provinces— small Bavarian towns, little seaside villages in Schleswig-Holstein—and yet when had the world come to hear of it? When those artists had traveled to Berlin!

The lecture continued later in Wilhelm's room. Toward twilight, when Wilhelm noted that the administration had scheduled an orientation tea, Hans responded that he had called for another hansom. They were going to Berlin for an orientation of their own.

The hansom deposited them at a streetcar stop. The streetcar arrived in minutes. Following Hans onto it, Wilhelm remembered the way he'd planned to go into Berlin after a month or so of settling into school and working up his courage.

Had Hans been to Berlin before? Wilhelm asked. His family was from the Grunewald, Hans answered. Then, respecting either his friend's embarrassment or excitement, he kept silent.

The streetcar rattled into the city center as the lamps were coming on. Along a row of bakeries, middle-aged men were hauling up their awnings and getting out their bicycles. The streetcar passed four-story homes flanked with ancient chestnut trees, and luxury hotels with names done up in electric lights—the Adlon, the Bristol, Horcher's. Lunchrooms and beer and sausage emporiums. Bars for draymen and coal- and potato-dealers. It stopped opposite the Komische Oper, which featured a twin bill of *Damnation: 1,000 Women!* and *Berlin Without a Blouse.*

They disembarked on the Leipzigerstrasse near Thälmannplatz, neither of them speaking. Wilhelm noted the location as if he'd be following a trail of bread crumbs home.

In an antiquities shop, they saw a display of prehistoric bones of the sort dug up in Asiatic deserts, then they walked slowly down a long, dim arcade, reading posters in the half-light.

For dinner, Hans debated with himself: Austro-Hungarian, Czech, or Russian. He chose a Russian café that was a favorite of his mother's, and there they stuffed themselves to the brim with cold eggplant slices in oil, miniature Siberian dumplings in broth, a pink lamb shashlik and, for dessert, *kisel,* an opaque fruit jell.

After dinner, Wilhelm's host announced that they were going to the All-City Revue *You've Gotta See It!* After paying the check, he led Wilhelm on a winding ramble which terminated at a huge dirty cellar that Wilhelm's father, Herr Plumpe, would have called a Low Place.

The crowd was bumptious and jovial. The first skit turned out to be a celebration of the new elevated trolley. Then some Hohenzollern statues somewhere were ridiculed in a kind of comic dumb-show. Then a female personification of the city sang "I have the foibles of my youth, I'm still a young metropolis!" And then a woman dressed as a cross between a sailor and a Catholic Cardinal—"Claire Waldoff!" Hans exclaimed as she emerged from behind the curtain to cheers—sang "Anyone Who's Reflected on These Times Will See: Everything Our Dads Respected Seems to Us Stupidity." The whole thing was tatty and absurd. The crowd sang along and offered alternative lyrics. Wilhelm was exhilarated. Everyone around him seemed to be the ultimate Berliner.

His host told him afterwards that they were probably all from Gelsenkirchen.

Outside, Hans announced that he was hungry again, and pulled Wilhelm inside another café by the jacket and introduced him to *bouletten,* minced meatballs, which he said was a Berlin specialty. Pyramids of them trembled on heavy china plates on the counters. They were eaten at room temperature, slippery with onion and fat, along with sour cucumber pickles and hard rolls.

They returned to their rooms with eleven minutes to spare before bed check. In the hansom ride back, Friedrich Wilhelm Plumpe could not put into words what the evening had meant to him. It had been similar to how he'd imagined storms in the tropics progressed: from exhaustion and terror to exhilaration and exaltation. The whole way back they barely spoke. Occasionally Hans smiled to himself, and when they arrived, he refused to let Wilhelm pay the fare.


A WEEK later Wilhelm was again pitched into a hansom, and this time taken to the Ehrenbaum-Degele home in the Grunewald for Sunday dinner.

The house was five stories high. The bottom floor was faced with antique fitted stone, the next two stories with granite, and the top two with Tudor paneling. In the center of the second story, the family initials were worked in iron and followed by an exclamation point. On one side, a dormer with two small attic windows and a large, arched window below created the effect of a house gaping at its approaching visitors. On the other, a stand of hundred-year-old pines extended into the forest. As they walked down the drive, Wilhelm felt unreasonable joy at the wealth of others.

They entered through a garden drowsy with sunlight. Wicker armchairs were arranged at intervals. A gardener dozed in a caved-in chair.

The house's sunroom was decorated with bowls of primroses and asters. The window frames were bright green. His host handed him a magazine, then went off to round up his father and mother. In the four corners were sprays of a dark red flower he could not identify. *The Fallen Warrior* from the Glyptothek confronted a Praxiteles *Hermes* on the mantel. Some contemporary paintings were lined up in box frames over the buffet table. Underneath, a dog, an Alsatian, lay asleep. Each paw constricted alternately, as if it were playing the piano.

The Ehrenbaum-Degeles made their entrance. Hans's father was the portrait of the prosperous Jewish banker. He had the expression of someone who, having discovered some minor embezzling, had decided to overlook it. When introduced, he transformed that into a warm smile and a searching look. He shook his guest's hand once, firmly, and introduced himself as Herr Ehrenbaum.

The mother introduced herself as Mary Degele, and insisted on "Mary." She was two inches taller than her husband, with her son's large-boned features and the sort of hair one saw in Biedermeier prints. From her first glance at Hans it was clear that her devotion was for her an unshakeable source of satisfaction.

Both parents were pleased to hear that their guest had admired Mary onstage, as Lucia. She engaged Wilhelm immediately with questions about school, and they all arranged themselves on some Swedish chairs. He answered the questions as best he could. He found he could not move his eyes from her.

She had a genius for making herself comfortable. She seemed to have developed a quietly sexual relationship with her divan. Servants came and went with trays, but amid whatever flurry and agitation, her face was a calm sea. Her expression, when she listened, suggested infinite patience. The lines of her throat were very beautiful. Wilhelm made a note to remark to Hans later that the pictures of Winterhalter were very much like her.

The cook escorted Hans's grandmother, who seemed no more

frail than Bismarck, out to the group. She said her hellos and settled beside her grandson on an ottoman. He kissed her cheek and
said, "Why don't you tell Wilhelm about your Parisian artist?
Only don't say a word about the Prussian whorehouse; you'll ruin
the family reputation."

The grandmother turned to Wilhelm and said placidly, "He
teases me."

Hans lowered his head to her breast like a horse and she
ruffled his hair. Taking his ease, he seemed to Wilhelm the epit-
ome of all those welcomed and sheltered by their families.

They talked away the afternoon. Mary Degele led them
through an appreciation of Furtwängler and the Philharmonic.
(The family had just been to see the Glorious Seventh, and some
Brahms.) Had Wilhelm ever had the opportunity to hear
Furtwängler's Seventh? No, he had not. She handled his chagrin
graciously, explaining the maestro's greatness with wry and
demystifying anecdotes, and then, with the artlessness of someone asking him to appreciate a beautiful day, invited him to be
their guest in the future.

The cook came back out and lit the lamps. The family heard
the story of how the boys had met. On the subject of their aspira-
tions, Wilhelm held forth in a way that was inconceivable in his
own home. In this house, apparently, he had courage. He argued
for the sublimity of the theater: for the deeper pleasure of moving
people directly, in person, and seeing the emotions of one's own
soul entering theirs. Hans argued for the supremacy of the written word and for the writer's pleasure of moving others across
time and space. When in support of that notion he recited from
Rilke, Wilhelm was entranced by the quality of the family's attention.

Herr Ehrenbaum took part in the discussion, encouraged his
son in whatever point he was making, and took evident pleasure
in what his wife was about to contribute.

Hans's grandmother announced that she had run out of energy, and Wilhelm wondered if it was time to go. In lieu of asking, he admired aloud a print of the Belvedere by Winckelmann. Mary Degele discussed its acquisition, and remarked on the sensuality of the south, in contrast to the prudishness of the north. Wilhelm felt himself blushing in response, despite all furious attempts to stop.

Once again the boys got back to school just in time to dash through their toilet prior to bed check. That night, listening to the snores and whimpers of his fellow neophytes, Wilhelm remembered her hair and her manner and thought, *That's my real university. That's where I'll learn everything I need to know.*

FRIEDRICH WILHELM PLUMPE had been raised in silence and routine in a cool blue nursery at the beginning of a comfortable era in his family's fortunes. Who understood him? His mother; his brothers. Then, not even them. His early childhood had been Westphalian, meaning that blank pastureland on which enormous, coarse-boned farmers raised ponderous draft horses, and the Plumpes had lived in a town so quiet that when Wilhelm looked out a window and finally did see a passerby, it was as if a tapestry had moved.

When he was five, they moved to Kassel, which his father saw as a fitting residence for the well-to-do man of independent means. Earlier his father had taken over an uncle's textile firm, and then sold it at an obvious profit. Wilhelm had been born in the Three Emperor Year of 1888, a few months after the coronation of Wilhelm II. Two years later, the Kaiser had designated Kassel as his summer residence. Wilhelm's father had immediately settled them in the vicinity of the palace, in the villa colony of Mulang.

There Herr Plumpe searched for his entry into society. The neighboring families were all nouveau-riche. There were mutual invitations to garden parties and Italianate evenings with lights and fireworks. Hosts were expected to provide fresh surprises for each gathering. But established society insulated itself against intrusions from below. This wounded Herr Plumpe profoundly. He withdrew to his study to plan newer and more efficient siege-towers.

In his view, the children's part of the house was an appendix, necessary during domestic crises that could not be settled without his intervention, but otherwise a desert to be crossed in great strides. Moreover, Wilhelm embodied for him his family's failure to fit in. His frailest son, useless in rough games, was a boy who, when banished to a field because the day was so glorious, would sit across from romping playmates on a portable folding chair, reading and not allowing himself to be distracted by the shouting.

Both father and son possessed an ocean of words, and in each other's presence became mute. In his father's view, words served as a confirmation of things, a sign of possession. To Wilhelm, they were foretastes of excitements barely glimpsed.

His father understood him to be like those boys who developed passions for trifles in order to persuade themselves that they were living poetically. His father's hope was to attend decisively to his still-unformed character. For stretches he could forgive his son. A member of the oldest family in town might single the boy out in public with an award for recitation, and Herr Plumpe's pride would allow him a respite. But then, when the expected invitation to that home failed to materialize, he again would be oppressed by the realization that his plans were precarious or collapsing, and once more the fury would be upon him. They were never Prussian enough. His wife finally found the courage to point out to him that the reason why was no mystery, since they weren't Prussian at *all*.

But Wilhelm was the least Prussian of them. On that, at least, everyone could agree.

So the angular and gawky Wilhelm ran errands as a pretext for getting out of the house. Sometimes he pretended to have forgotten something so he could go out again. In the tradition of boys in this position, he devoured adventure stories, particularly those set in the tropics. No illustration was too crudely colored, no story too absurd for his guilty appetite. When he ran out of books, he visited the galleries in town, assembled over the previous century by the Hessian Dukes. He haunted the Court Theater, absorbing its classical repertoire. He wandered the house mangling snippets of Shakespeare, Schiller, Goethe, Lessing, and Grillparzer. On weekends he was allowed to attend performances that ended near midnight. (A boy in attendance alone was no cause for concern, since the theater's explicit purpose was moral uplift.)

What a privilege theatergoing seemed to be! To be left alone in the dark, no one asking him questions, the king of his seat, content to let everything pass before him. There he felt the return of that part of himself that had to slink away each day so that another part could remain behind to enjoy his family.

At the dinner table his father might fulminate every so often at yet another day his son had wasted. While he did so, his wife gazed on the passing storm in her usual meditative and not unpleasant trance. But Wilhelm's privileges, as his brothers bitterly noted, remained unrevoked. The Would-be Artist, they complained, expected and received from all others, but especially from their mother, preferential treatment because of his Temperament. Nerves, his brother Bernhard sourly called it. So that even before Wilhelm separated himself from that world—even before he rid himself of what he felt to be the oafishness of "Plumpe" and thus made a visible, official break with that past—he had begun to draw back from it, and it had continued its process of drawing away from him.

AND WHAT did he retain of philology? Of those sleepy mornings and afternoons in ruined old classrooms, with the brocades and wainscoting disintegrating in the damp? That everything seemed prefatory to outings with Hans.

Wilhelm traded one authority disappointed in him for others, from his father to Dr. Krefeld—whose every sentence began "Well, so . . ."—to Dr. Widmann, who drifted desk to desk only to pivot suddenly on one foot to launch a question in an unexpected direction.

For the most part, he sat through all of it dull, moony, and silent, interested only in their rhetorical exercises, in which those called upon could be Frederick, or Vercingetorix, or Caesar. Performing these roles, he felt Protean; he entered the thoughts of other men, and understood that each made decisions according to his own laws.

What he loved most were the exercise-walks, he and Hans taking their places behind the others and chattering like birds. Here they embroidered upon the theme of what they'd accomplish once they left school. To begin with, they would go on a long voyage. The thought of that sustained them through all sorts of unpleasantness. Usually they reprised the group walk on their own later in the day. They'd walk for miles. A feeling of suffocation would overcome them, and they'd lie dazed on their backs in a field. Then they'd return and again climb the stairs to their rooms, feeling as sad as if they'd indulged in a wild debauchery. One of their professors maintained that they overexcited each other.

In the evenings they worked together, their studies interrupted by remarks, jokes, confidences, and half-serious arguments. If one of them napped, the other resumed his studies. They composed pantheons and contradicted themselves regularly, their prejudices in a highly confused state. They were jealous of mutual friends. They were each other's ideal audience. "We saw you two on the street this morning," classmates told them. "What on earth was the joke?"

One twilight they sat through a downpour at an outdoor café, covering their coffees with their palms, soaked to the skin. After the rain had stopped, a sinister young waiter murmured, "Plenty of young ladies around this evening, gentlemen."

At times, Hans was so relaxed in his presence that he fell asleep on streetcars. His kindness was so disarming that Wilhelm planned his gifts weeks in advance.

Before meeting Wilhelm, he had strived to model himself on the calm good sense and honesty of Xenophon. He'd cried upon first reading the passage in the *Anabasis* when the vanguard of the column reached the summit and finally caught sight of the sea. He left notes on Wilhelm's bed: *Thought more about your remarks re Langbehn. Felt I gave them short shrift. More to come. H.* His presence educated even when he was silent.

Goethe claimed that there were two ways in which a man might dare to be himself: prayer and song. Wilhelm had always assumed he had the capacity for neither, and that his most intense and important affections would go through life with their eyes turned away. For him, Hans became a third option. But even if their time together seemed a journal of obstructed fortune and unfulfilled wishes, he believed the icy surface of his own priggishness was beginning to darken, crack, and give way to the fluid cold layers beneath.


AT THAT point, as was customary with overheated boys at a certain level of higher learning, Goethe prevailed. The two had spent an entire month trailing Dr. Widmann through the trackless moors of *Faust*. The poem had seized their imagination to such an extent that they began to term their walks *Faust*-walks.

The *Faust*-walks led to new possibilities for the covert discussion of unapproachable subjects. They might remark upon Faust's life as a story of the protracted and perverse disregard for the obvious, or note that his longing for escape mirrored the wish to break free of the isolation of being himself. This sort of talk so excited them that finally they planned a day-trip to the mountains. The preceding week they saw little of each other, as if husbanding nervous energy. Who knew what could happen on such an outing?

They took the train as far as Zwickau. There, high on the slopes, far from even the hiking-tracks, they surrounded themselves with fire lilies, purple gentians, and alpine columbines. They had vistas at their feet. Their talk was full of sobriety and foolishness. In the original *Faust*, they agreed, there were two peaks of emotion: his turning from God to the Devil, and his last hours awaiting damnation. Yet Goethe had added a third peak, in the center, with the kiss that sealed Faust's love for Gretchen—her story integral to the theme of damnation because Faust's claim of freedom from moral restrictions had the potential for tragic guilt. In support of that interpretation, Hans reminded Wilhelm that Goethe himself had brutally terminated his first affair, with Friederike Brion.

When they unpacked their lunch, Hans's cucumber sandwich had spoiled. During the intervals of silence, they blushed. The game-playing exacerbated their prickliness and desire. Movement off in the flowers made them jump.

Faust was stubborn, they decided, unwilling to lose any part of himself. He did not know how to renounce. Goethe's greatest verses concerned the abyss between the desires of which he felt himself composed and the world in which those desires needed to be realized. Lying shoulder to shoulder, breathing in the hot wind sweeping up from the valley, they nearly levitated from tension. A warbler landed nearby and moved forward hop by cautious hop, its sharp round eye holding them in view.

The intensity of Faust's desire for Gretchen, up to that point imprisoned in the iron bands of his heart, had overwhelmed the simple and well-tried vices offered by Mephistopheles. In her face Faust had seen innocence, and the possibility of goodness within "the constricted life." The supreme moment of his life on earth, which had passed away as it came into being, had been when Gretchen had returned his kiss and made her own declaration, addressing him as *du* rather than *Sie*.

The sun heated the grasses around them. Their agitation alternated with intoxication. A fly drew figure-eights over Hans's face, and Wilhelm shooed it away. Hans's skin shared the bitter freshness of the columbines. The silence was jostled by the browsings of a cow whose role it was to appear and disappear from sight.

Even when sharing confidences, they came upon cliffs which brought them to a halt. They weren't sure they'd be understood. It was difficult to express anything with the required precision.

An hour later, they hiked down the mountain, still talking like pedants. They settled for the cold comfort of double meanings. Faust's insight into intimacy came *as a result of* his congress with infernal powers: the lover was inseparable from the pact-maker with the Devil. Hence the reaction of a social order as merciless as Mephistopheles himself. Hence the remorseless approach of public shame. Hence her final words to him: *Mute lies the world, like the grave!*

On the train back to Charlottenburg they rode third class. A few seats down, a girl sat perfectly composed, a hand on each thigh. The boy beside her looked out the window. "Watch," Hans remarked quietly, with no preface. "They don't even glance at one other. They continue touching, as if by accident. Watch how alert they are. How excited."

"They're already in each other's arms, in bed," he added. Across from them, an elderly woman cleared her throat.

That night Wilhelm made both sides of the pillow hot. He dressed and took a long walk, encountering other headache experts on their wanderings.

He decided on a plan of action that would bury him in his studies.

A week later, he and Hans stayed out all night in the city. At dawn they found themselves in a dismal precinct, in a wilderness of railway lines. Chimneys and warehouses took on distinct outlines in the distance. They climbed a tall, rusty trestle. Sounds from a nearby market lifted up to them. A milk bottle on stone, the crank of an awning, a cart wheeled slowly across cobblestone. Beneath them, out for their own walk, a man and a woman picked their way over the railroad ties. They talked in hushed tones and shared a cigarette. And Hans put his full lips on Wilhelm's mouth, kissed him, and turned away.

THAT HAD not been Wilhelm's first sexual experience. On his fourteenth birthday his father had called him into his study to announce that Wilhelm would be having a party, and to request a list of girls that might be invited. He'd been pleased when his son had been able to name two immediately: Emmy Virchov, who knew so much about poetry and always teased him; and Rose Siedhoff, a Jewess keen on music and painting, very soft-spoken and a great favorite of his mother's. Herr Plumpe had asked for more names. Emmy and Rose had been an acceptable beginning but also oversensitive and odd. And neither was pretty.

Wilhelm had had no more names. Additional names had been provided by his brothers. The evening had not been a success: a gathering of solitaires politely weathering the noise until they could again be left alone with their books.

That summer his parents took him to the island of Juist in the North Sea, partly for a change of air, and also to stop his hiding indoors and reading. He was by then officially delicate. There was less conflict at the beach, because he loved the dunes, and swimming.

On that island, to the astonishment of his family, he formed an acquaintance with a fisherman who every day crossed back and forth in a ketch in front of the beach. The fisherman put in at a nearby inlet, and young Wilhelm walked over to him and struck up a conversation. The fisherman took him sailing. Herr Plumpe was openmouthed. When the boat rounded the headland and the beach fell out of sight, the fisherman dropped the sail, let the boat drift, and opened the buttons of his pants. He showed Wilhelm what he wanted. As if paralyzed, Wilhelm lay in the thwarts. He noticed that one of his hands remained outspread throughout. He saw stars. He wanted to do this every day.

On their return, they ran their boat aground a few feet from Herr Plumpe's lounge-chair. The fisherman told Herr Plumpe that the boy had a talent for sailing. Every day afterwards, until the family left the island, he and Wilhelm would sail around the headlands, drop the sail, and pull each other free of their pants, letting themselves drift.

FOLLOWING THEIR kiss, they spent the day in Wilhelm's room embracing and kissing in passionate fits and starts but refraining from anything else. In situations like this, Hans said, he imagined a man hiding in the wardrobe, ready to make him pay through the nose for the rest of his life. When Wilhelm broached the subject of amorous adventures in general, he declared both his pity for the ravages of passion and his revulsion at hypocrisy. They both spoke as seasoned men of the world, between kisses that made them tilt and lean on an unsteady floor.

THEY RETURNED to class the next day, their absence loudly noted for the group by one of their classmates, a boy named Walter Spiess.

Spiess they'd registered from the beginning as having a face that looked to have been modeled in a confectioner's shop. They knew him as a saboteur capable of demoralizing an entire class. His poem on the battle of Actium had won the monthly prize, even though it had flaunted the fact that after its first two lines— *Spindle-topped waves / hurl themselves at the sea-chariots*—it had had nothing whatsoever to do with the subject. In the dramatic club he had played Hecate, called upon to witness Wilhelm's oath, as Jason, to Hans's Medea.

He watched them from a distance for the few weeks following their day-long absence and then, one afternoon, asked them to look at one of his paintings. It was a catastrophe, he shrugged, but they'd get an idea of what he did. There was a blankness to his manner which was not simplicity. He seemed to be committed to nothing in particular, to stand in an attitude of general hospitality to opportunities.

He and Hans led the way. Wilhelm followed, feeling excluded and faintly sulky.

Spiess's room was at the end of a hallway, half hidden beneath a staircase. They were impressed by what he'd done with it. He'd found an antique bronze screen for his fireplace, and had brought in a Turkish divan. In an alcove he'd constructed a sultan's tent of pink silk and muslin. Inside, over the bed, a small silver casket hung suspended by chains.

His easels were in the bathtub. His landscapes turned out to involve monstrous trees that confronted one another over prostrate figures. Over the sink he'd framed a medieval woodcut of a witches' sabbath. The artist had conceived it as a cross between a carnival and a trade convention. Arty newspapers—*Free Spirit, The Herald of Hellas, New Friendship*—were spread around the floor.

After a short visit they left, and made no subsequent overtures. Even so, they got to know him. He surfaced wherever they went, always scratching around about money; he'd changed his mind about a tutoring job when his future charge had asked in a peculiar way if he was interested in poisonous spiders. He had terrible luck with clothes, and his favorite hat had to be thrown away after he got sick into it one night at the theater.

He also announced himself to be a democratizing influence. Concerning the arts, he pretended to be bored to tears by all pretension: the ballet should be forbidden by the Reichstag; for entertainment there were boxing matches and bicycle races; if anyone needed more, they should stay at home and look in the mirror. He represented, he told them, all that was best in the modern consciousness. He kept a pair of opera glasses in his room, through which he looked at a nudist in an apartment across the street. The man was fat and would go about his business in the evenings with the curtains open, reading and handling himself. About sex it became evident that he had the matter-of-factness of someone sitting down to dinner.

Wilhelm and Hans agreed to remain polite but not welcoming. One night, two months after they'd climbed the railway trestle, Spiess stopped by Wilhelm's room, when Hans was at the library, to ask if he wished to go for a walk. Wilhelm declined but was intrigued. And Hans was late. An hour went by. Restless and annoyed, Wilhelm decided to go to the library. He left his room thinking of Spiess, then turned a corner and ran into him.

Their impulse was to draw back, but they went up to each other. As if by agreement, they walked around the school grounds and the athletic fields.

They talked about their backgrounds. Spiess complimented him on his height. Wilhelm mentioned in turn that he'd liked the sultan's tent. He was titillated by the decadence of the flirtation, yet berated himself. Wasn't he devoted to someone else? Didn't he have any rules? Would the few he tried to impose upon himself constantly give way? Suppose Hans returned? Where would he say he'd been? He walked along, hands in pockets, absorbed with the complications. The idea of causing Hans pain appalled and fascinated him. He was a small boy considering the effects of shaking the ant-farm. What a pig I am, he finally thought, glorying in his wickedness.

# BERLIN,
# 1910

I T  W A S  characteristic of Hans that the first afternoon they spoke, he asked Wilhelm his goals in life. Wilhelm surprised himself by answering "The theater," and from thereafter philology receded rapidly. A year later they quit Charlottenburg together to study art history and literature in Heidelberg. When Spiess wrote, offering to visit, they never responded.

In Heidelberg as students they performed Schiller in the presence of the Grand Duke of Baden. Max Reinhardt was in the audience. Backstage he sought out Hans and Wilhelm, still in costume, and offered the nineteen-year-old Wilhelm a place in his newly founded theater school in Berlin. If he agreed to stay for six years, it would cost nothing. Wilhelm was nonplussed. Hans said, "He accepts your offer right here, on the spot." For years afterwards Reinhardt referred to Hans as Wilhelm's "agent."

Wilhelm's father was not informed. The arrangement had been for him to send the money for the term-bills directly to his son, and Wilhelm simply had his mail forwarded. It took his father a year to discover what was happening. He had premonitions of trouble, though; every so often he sent along with the tuition money a postcard on which was written *Domi manere felicibus convenit:* The happy do best to stay at home.


W H A T  A  corps Reinhardt had collected! The evening of the introductory lecture, they attended a reception hosted by Reinhardt at his home. Their invitation read, "Herr Plumpe and his Agent." They met Müthel, Hoffman, Storm, Eckersberg, Conrad Veidt,

Granach, and Lubitsch. Reinhardt himself never joined the party. At various points he emerged backlit on the upper landing of the darkened staircase, a shadowy presence overseeing the proceedings.

Everyone turned out to be one of Reinhardt's discoveries. Eckersberg he'd noticed in a church choir. Lubitsch had been a tailor's apprentice. Within a half hour of their arrival, the new recruits had bonded sufficiently to create an imbroglio by defending Granach, a stumpy Jew from Galicia, from the anti-Semitic teasing of one of the instructors.

They felt exhilarated and full of themselves. Appreciably taller than the rest, Veidt and Wilhelm regarded each other over a sea of heads. They'd been the most strenuous in the skirmish over Granach. Hans christened them "the two bell-towers."

Veidt was striking: gaunt and pallid, with a drawn face that gave people an uncomfortable sense of the skull beneath. He reminded Wilhelm of something that might hang at a crossroads in winter. His humor was quiet and mordant. His eyes worked to insure that no one outdid his tragic or sinister air. He wore nothing but black.

They exhausted one another's backgrounds and stood about in nervous groups, gossiping in low voices, watching the stairs for Reinhardt's reappearance. They noted what hung on the walls. They nibbled goose and liver sausage. They traded enthusiasms about a legendary production of *A Midsummer Night's Dream* which each of them had seen three years earlier: the curtain going up on real trees, growing not out of painted ground-cloth but of palpable grass! Real flowers embowering the middle distance, the beeches and lake in the background mirrored between two hills. A moon shining over real mist. Streams trickling. And just when they'd believed they had absorbed the production's visual wonder, the stage had begun to revolve. The gasp from the audience! The entire forest slowly revealed new aspects and perspectives inexhaustible as nature. Elves and fairies darted through the scene, disappearing behind trees, re-emerging from hillocks. Who could doubt Lysander's bewilderment in such a setting? The opening moment had expressed the very heart of the play.

Speaking of gasps from the audience, Veidt said, and went on to tell them the first story they'd heard of the poet Else Lasker-Schüler: her scandal the year before in the company's production of *The Moor's Seraglio*.

She'd maneuvered herself an extra's role as one of the lovers carried onstage in pairs and reclining on litters during the climactic scene in the courtesans' quarters. Each night her litter was deposited against the back wall of the set, as downstage a sword-fight was staged in front of a dazzling corps de ballet. In the middle of the play's run, she'd informed Veidt that on her litter every night she made love with her partner, a young masseuse from the Saar named Anni, who wore an appliance she warmed and lubricated beforehand. Each night Anni opened her robe and they began while still being carried on, held above their slaves' heads.

Veidt and his pals Granach and Lubitsch had appeared at the next performance armed with the best opera glasses they could find. They confirmed her story. They then attended performances on seven consecutive nights, bringing with them an ever-increasing group of theater lovers. Lasker-Schüler and her Anni mounted each other throughout the scene, concealed by the fact that the other pairs of lovers were miming the same activity. Later, she told Veidt that each night when the curtain came down, they separated, flushed and focused on their own pleasure, changed side by side in the chaos of the extras' dressing room, absorbed in their mirrors, not allowing themselves to touch. Then they rendezvoused in the basement costume-storerooms, nesting on gowns and hussars' capes arranged in a crate.

Reinhardt had finally noticed, and fired her. In her poems afterwards she'd referred to her "Turkish Anni."

Upon hearing the story, Hans resolved that she should attend one of his parents' soirées.

After Reinhardt's party the new recruits went out to certain clubs of Veidt's choosing. Wilhelm and Hans hesitated, but were titillated by what they might see, since Berlin, for them, meant Boys. Before leaving for school, Wilhelm had spent sleepless nights flipping through an underground guide to Berlin, subtitled *What Baedeker Won't Tell You.*

The first club was in an unmarked subbasement on a deserted street. Veidt led the way, their scoutmaster. Granach, Müthel, Hans, and Wilhelm followed. Inside the outer door was a heavy leather curtain; Wilhelm was the last one through once Veidt swept it aside. The group stood around like a hiking club that had stumbled onto a ladies' tea.

The cement floor had been painted black, the lights blue. The effect was that of an aquarium twilight.

The patrons returned to what they were doing. What they were doing, Veidt explained as his charges crowded into two high-backed benches separated by a filthy wooden table, was violating §180, §74, and §183 of the Criminal Code.

The long and narrow room was decorated with articles of clothing, most of which they couldn't identify. A mockery of a rustic sign hung over the beer taps, and the table coasters were labeled Cozy Corner. A *Polizeiknüppel,* a leather-covered length of steel spring, hung on the wall behind the bartender.

At the far end, a raised platform was flanked by two dwarf spotlights and a curtain.

At the nearest table, a boy dressed without conviction as a sailor sat with a man in English tweeds. They kissed. The sailor eased the Oxford don's lips apart with two fingers.

"My God," Granach said from deep in their booth, and Veidt excused himself to chat with someone at the bar.

Boys who sold themselves for sex, Müthel finally remarked, had no future. They all looked at him.

"The voice of experience," Hans said.

Nevertheless, Müthel said. It was true. Their clients couldn't allow themselves to care what became of them.

They abused him for his threepenny psychology, and in so doing led themselves out of their paralysis of excitement and terror.

It occurred to them that they were thirsty. They tried various ways of attracting the barkeep's attention.

Granach ventured the opinion that since prostitution was heartless and marriage immoral, abstention was preferable. Müthel added that he regarded women as a distraction, nothing more. Hans took both their hands, and said, "Come, now. Why don't we all face the music and say what we mean: that we're frankly afraid of them?"

Wilhelm kept to himself, aware that he didn't know how anyone besides merchants' sons and bookworms actually spoke.

Veidt stood at the bar sipping champagne. He looked to be considering the clientele with unsurprised benevolence.

Granach mentioned that he'd first seen Veidt in a cabaret on the Schützenstrasse. Veidt had played The Doomed Homosexual. That had been at least two years ago. How old could he have been?

Müthel wanted to know if they thought he was a member of—what was it called?—the Society of Free Spirits.

Wilhelm looked at Hans and Hans looked away. He seemed relaxed.

Granach shrugged, then put two coasters over his eyes for monocles. What was that gang on about, anyway? he asked.

Müthel said that, as he understood it, the idea was the celebration of Greek ideals. Spiritual calm and inner peace, in the intimate company of a friend.

Oh, yes, Granach said. Willi and Fritzi, after the football match. The older and younger boy at school. *The evening tutorial, in which the most spiritual of values were inculcated . . . Willi had dropped his pen-knife in Fritzi's bed, and together they hunted for it, for without it there would be no fun that day."*

Hans smiled across the table at Wilhelm: a calming, beautiful smile.

Where was the barkeep? Müthel wanted to know. Were they ever going to drink?

In the penultimate chapter, the inevitable discovery, Granach added. Handled with more *tristesse* than panic: *"But the strict Head-master found out their inclinations."*

Hans smiled again. It sounded, he said, like Granach had done some hunting for the pen-knife himself.

Granach laughed.

The conversation lapsed.

Veidt finally returned, easing in beside Wilhelm so that their bodies touched from shoulder to knee. Granach asked if this so-called bar in fact ever served anything to drink. Veidt asked what they'd been talking about. Müthel caught him up on the conversation.

" 'The sordid perils of actual existence,' " Veidt remarked, looking at Wilhelm.

Hans regarded them both.

"Granach was telling us about your role as The Doomed Homosexual," Müthel said.

"As to questions concerning my nature," Veidt said, with a smile, "my usual answer is 'Musical.' "

The bartender arrived with a tray of five glasses of Mampe's orange-flavored cordial.

"Who ordered these?" Granach asked.

"Whom do you think?" Veidt said.

They toasted themselves.

"What are we?" Granach asked, grimacing at the taste. "Eng-lish shopkeepers' wives?"

"A man over there gave me his card," Veidt said, removing it from a pocket and showing it round. "It says under his name, 'Portuguese Doctor.' "

"As in Dutch wife?" Hans asked. "French letter? Spanish fly?"

The two dwarf spotlights at the end of the bar flared on, and a fanfare was performed by a fat man with a clarinet. He then pulled open the curtain to reveal two women in heavy makeup and dressed as Amazons. The special quality of the proceedings that followed depended in part on the disparity in the size of the women. One was so small as to appear to be the other's daughter. They mimed a pitched battle which ended with the tiny woman pinned, at which point they seemed to see each other with new eyes. The victor lowered her face slowly, while the vanquished kept her eyes on the approaching mouth. At the crucial moment the victor stopped, their open lips only grazing. The group at the table could hear breathing, and glasses clinking. Then the victor reared back and tore away the tunic from between the vanquished's legs. The vanquished did the same to the victor. The fat man performed another fanfare. Neither woman was a woman.

The victor began to lower his mouth toward the proof of the vanquished's masculinity.

The group at the table seemed unwilling to breathe. Wilhelm felt like he had become afflicted with a new, pleasurable form of fever.

The lights went out and a cheer rose up from the patrons. When the lights came back up, the two principals were holding hands and taking bows.

Veidt got up while they were still applauding. Time to get out of here, he said. They had other stops to make.

Out on the street, he fell into step beside Wilhelm and asked if that was the first male organ Wilhelm had seen in public. Ahead of them, Hans strode with his hands in his pockets, forcing Müthel to trot every so often to keep up.

Wilhelm could easily have called to him.

The next club was as raucous as a rally. A paralyzed patron, wheeled up a ramp onto the stage, dictated his will to wild applause. A grateful young man in silk trousers the color of pomegranate climbed onto his lap and passed cherries to him mouth to mouth while the crowd whooped like Red Indians. After each transfer the paralyzed man would chew the cherry and spit the pit high out into the audience.

The club after that featured two veiled tableaus: "Victory in Her Golden Chariot" and "The Shame of Catherine the Great." While the latter was assembling itself, Hans touched Wilhelm's shoulder and pointed. Spiess was along the opposite wall, sitting by himself. He gave no sign of having seen them.

With the evening winding down, Veidt read their palms. Hans's left hand revealed a few simple gifts, and his right promised them rich development. The opposite proved the case with Wilhelm's hands: many gifts, destined to go unused.

While his hand was still in Veidt's, Spiess passed their table.

On the way to the streetcar stop Granach took Wilhelm aside and mentioned that Veidt was someone who let his little head rule his big head.

Rattling along on the streetcar, they talked about Byron. The saddest thing about his early death, Hans volunteered, was the way it overshadowed his work in so many memories.


WILHELM'S EDUCATION with Reinhardt proceeded. He worked on chamber-pieces adapted from Lessing. He was added to small committees Reinhardt called problem-groups to work on specific issues involved in the staging.

The first was lighting. This was his introduction to Reinhardt's *Kuppelhorizont,* a plaster cyclorama sky-dome attached to a cupola that overhung the back of the stage. The plaster was covered with a kind of glaze. Properly lit with a diffused and modulated light, it transformed itself into a stunning illusion of space, and infinite depth.

He found himself astounded by the possibilities. Reinhardt dropped in every so often to monitor his team's progress or gently urge them in one direction or another. They taught themselves all about light. They were drunk with light.

So that for their first production, the curtain rose on a horizon flooded with ultramarine moonlight. Then the theater was plunged into darkness, until a magic lantern in the orchestra pit, manipulated by a crouching Granach turning and turning his crank, covered the sky with rushing opalescent clouds.

Wilhelm and his group became the celebrated lighting-masters. *Hamlet* opened later that year with shadowy figures high on dark battlements against a bleak North Sea sky. *Macbeth* the following summer opened with witches in translucent costumes backlit by a sunset so fiery that they resembled agile skeletons dancing.

Their sunsets or northern skies could fill with or be drained of light at will because Reinhardt had invented, while Wilhelm's group had watched and experimented and contributed whatever it could, what he called the "lighting console," a large plywood board of interconnected and labeled switches which the operator could play like a musical instrument, bringing up light in the east even as he faded stars in the west.

VISITING BERLIN, one of his brother's friends saw Wilhelm in a small role in *Hamlet*. He was using an anagrammatic stage name but was recognized because of his height and his hair, which he'd left red for the part.

His father sent a three-line postcard. *Nothing. Not another pfennig. I paid for you to become a professor, not a starving actor.* The cheques stopped.

After Murnau had written a number of letters, Frau Plumpe worked out a solution. *Her* father would continue the support. Her husband would never find out.

Wilhelm's brother eventually wrote that every so often their father would ask how he was managing up in Berlin, and their mother would assume a prim and displeased expression and say only "He's managing."

Once he got what he wanted, he wrote less and less. His mother's letters became more plaintive, and despite her pain, his remained unapologetic, and rare.

ABOUT THAT time, they made their acquaintance of the famous Lasker-Schüler by attending one of her poetry readings. Wilhelm invited Veidt along but Veidt said he'd had enough histrionics for the day. Hans was sulky when he heard, and Wilhelm let him sulk.

When they arrived at the Romanische Café, Lasker-Schüler was seated by herself near the door of the ladies' room. Her eyes were closed, her fingertips held to her temples. She was small, with short hair. Her velvet jacket was the same brilliant red as her lips, and despite the season she wore wide Turkish pants and a Tartar's fur cap. She'd painted a golden arrow down her throat. The arrowhead echoed the vee of her buttoned blouse.

Hans pointed out a small boy sitting Indian-style on the floor, playing with a wooden glider. Waiters stepped over him.

Veidt had identified Paul, her son by her second husband.

Hans went over to him. Wilhelm kept his seat.

The boy looked asthmatic and pale and miserable in the smoke. He lifted the glider for Hans's inspection.

The master of ceremonies ascended the steps and banged the podium with the heel of his hand. Hans returned to his chair. Lasker-Schüler surfaced from her meditation and stepped onto the platform while the introduction was still proceeding.

The audience laughed affectionately. Apparently this was the sort of thing she did.

"Is that a street sign, Else?" someone called, referring to the arrow. There were boos and whistles and laughter.

"So often it's the woman in whom awareness resides," Lasker-Schüler said comfortably. "The man, stripped of his power, gazes on, inadequate."

Laughter and cheers.

Her first piece was a dialogue with a wood grouse. Wilhelm made a list of things to do for the next day. On the floor in front of his mother, Paul described loops in the air with his glider. Then, in a clear, full voice, she recited: *"Your sinful mouth's my burial crypt / Narcotic in its sweetness, fragrant-lipped, / So that my virtues fall asleep. / I drink with drunken senses from its well / And will-lessly, sink into its deep, / With radiant thoughts descending into hell. / My lips are parted in shy hesitation, / Like poisonous flowers that do the devil's bidding."*

AFTER THAT, the two friends saw her whenever she read anywhere within reach. Their enthusiasm continued unabated for nearly a year. Each occasion was different. One recital in a gallery was accompanied by bells, flutes, and a man who made occasional gasping sounds; for another she stood in a deep box while an assistant continually poured dirt over her. Her voice was insinuating, breathy, and expressive. At the end of every reading she came over to them, leading Paul by the hand. Hans became the only person with whom the boy seemed at ease.

She and Hans exchanged poems, and she proclaimed herself prostrate before his talent. She began calling him "Tristan." She dedicated poems to him, and was capable of producing one on the spot. Her first to Hans began *In your blue soul / The night places her stars.* In place of a hello, she took to reciting it with her eyes closed.

She was a bottomless source of gossip. She told spectacular and unlikely stories about the grandest figures. She interrogated Hans and Wilhelm about the True Place of Poetry and Theater in the modern world. She also held forth with intelligence and passion on Hans's writing. Her encouragement gave him great hope, and her patronage generated public readings and the interest of reputable publishers.

She struck Wilhelm at first as one of those annoying café artists always on the hunt for shattering emotional experiences. But when he ventured to share that opinion, Hans ignored him.

Whatever her weaknesses—and some of the poems, they agreed, testified to a total softening of the brain—Hans maintained that at a time in which the love poem had become an endangered anachronism, she'd restored the form to great beauty.

She talked and they listened, usually in cafés, with Paul asleep in Hans's lap, Hans stroking his hair. The poem, she believed, was nothing more than the poet's faulty record of the poetic state; she caught her breath in images. She tried to seduce Hans with the straightforwardness of someone going to market. She worked to enlist Wilhelm's help, and made use of Paul. Hans spent more time with her alone, at her request, and resisted her advances. They worked together on his poetry.

He'd come around, she told him. She admired what she imagined to be her own touching helplessness. By way of explanation, she said she'd noticed that even the roughest person was conquered by her fear.

Hans called her a child. She responded that she was always being called a child, and that making a child of someone was just as mysterious to her as making an angel of someone—it was like giving with one hand and taking with the other.

She didn't want a friend, Wilhelm finally told him. She wanted an unconditional surrender.

Hans chose not to answer. Then he said that what they both

connected with, when it came to Else, was that longing for a second face.


THEY RECEIVED in the post a handbill announcing Hans's inclusion in a New Poets reading series. Else Lasker-Schüler would introduce him.

Hans's writing occurred at all hours, day or night. He was able to start and stop at will. He wrote in longhand, looping in his amendations neatly and scratching out deletions with a razor.

Wilhelm had been his primary reader since they'd met. When he'd arrived at Charlottenburg, Wilhelm had considered one of his other callings to have been verse. Hans had expressed admiration for one poem, and had not asked to see another.

The reading was to be held in a common room attached to a Lutheran church in Mariendorf. The night of the reading they splurged and rode the whole route by taxi. Both were silent. Too excited to speak, Hans shuffled his recopied poems in a folder on his lap.

Paul greeted them at the door, wearing a small blue bow tie and holding a carnation for Hans. He was delighted he had something to give.

Three other poets were also on the program. They waited in separate corners to go on. They posed.

Lasker-Schüler said that her husband and some friends were coming.

They sat at the front of a few rows of empty folding chairs. The audience looked to consist of some local artists and a church usher who was keeping an eye on things.

The husband and friends never materialized. Eventually, Lasker-Schüler stopped waiting and announced they would begin. She stood and welcomed those in front of her.

Hans was first. Her introduction ran as follows: "Ladies and

Gentlemen, Spirits and Slaves, Sons of Moloch, I give you one of Heaven's Elect. I give you a Windstorm. I give you Hans Ehrenbaum-Degele."

The audience applauded as though they'd wait and see about that Windstorm.

But Hans read with the confidence and fluency of someone in the middle of a storied career. Standing up there alone with his few sheets of paper, he had more presence than Wilhelm had achieved in his years of shambling about onstage.

He read a series of lyrics in an order the two friends had debated. Three city poems first: "Rhapsody," "Not Yet Day! The Hideous Night—," and "Rejoicing Zion, Murderous Baal." Then a poem for Lasker-Schüler, followed by one for Wilhelm—"And There Will Be Days Like Silk"—and finally, an elegy entitled "My Friend, Who Went to the Shadows," which he refused to discuss.

The applause afterwards was sincere. That night they toasted the beginning of his public career as a poet. He soon was published in small magazines and the Sunday newspaper supplements, and made plans for a chapbook. He became known to other poets. "And There Will Be Days Like Silk" appeared in *Free Spirit,* with the dedication "For Ulrich the Helmet"—a nickname coined by Lasker-Schüler.

Even so, Wilhelm wondered about that mysterious Friend now in the Shadows. Had Hans meant him, or a rival?

He had little opportunity to find out. Reinhardt demanded more and more of his attention. But, as he wrote his mother, to be twenty years old and onstage with the sort of actors and actresses that had begun to crowd those productions . . . ! There would be time for talk later. And Hans had his own life. In the meantime, at any given night, in any production: Wegener, Basserman, Loos, Veidt, Krauss, or Jannings.

Of course all the other theater companies began pillaging

from them. All over Berlin, all over Germany, somewhere in Act I, young men emerged from the gloom like wraiths, while diagonals of light fell from high windows into vast and empty atriums. Every production began to look like theirs. And why not? Wilhelm himself was copying all he could, and in the process learning discernment, dedication, focus, and confidence. Reinhardt's confidence, as sets collapsed and experiments backfired and audiences mutinied, reminded Wilhelm of a remark attributed to Haydn while the French were besieging Vienna: *Don't worry. When Haydn's around, nothing can go wrong.*

He was learning Romanticism: in Reinhardt productions Expressionist screaming might be restaged as tender kisses. He was learning subtlety: Reinhardt taught him how to use the quieter characters onstage like those half-shaded figures behind the heroes who could so transform a painting.

He profited most from Reinhardt's method of keeping a Director's Book. Reinhardt worked on it for weeks before a production began, its purpose to give physical form to the text. Scenery, props, notes on character, changes of light, the volume and duration of the music—it was all there, in Reinhardt's crowded handwriting. And in just under eight months, twenty-year-old Wilhelm from Westphalia progressed from merely watching to being allowed his own entries.

Wilhelm saved, and framed, the program notes for *The Miracle,* in which he had his largest role, as The Knight. The program notes consisted of the title, the credits, and then eight sentences, boxed: *In our age we can communicate across the ocean. But the path to ourselves and our neighbor remains infinite. The actor walks this path. He transforms himself, his hands, eyes, and mouth full of miracles, and is at once artist and work of art. He lives at the border of reality. He carries in him the potential for all passions, for all fates, for all forms of inner life. He shows us that nothing human is foreign to us. If it were not so, we could not understand other men.*

. . .

HE SAW even less of Hans after they had an ugly argument over Wilhelm's handling of a letter from his mother. She had written that his father was doing badly, continually oppressed, furiously complaining that Wilhelm now belonged to that other hostile part of the world; that he couldn't count on his children to carry on his name.

What about his brothers? Wilhelm had wanted to know. Couldn't they deal with this? But Hans had been moved by the letter, and urged Wilhelm to visit. Wilhelm refused, though he finally wrote to Bernhard, his eldest brother, informing him of his decision to cut himself off. He told Hans a day later, elaborating with a little pride on his letter's language. Hans responded that the necessity of an event did not establish its virtue.


THEN LASKER-SCHÜLER brought them back together by staging a surprise party for Hans's birthday. Wilhelm was too absorbed in a new production to take part in the preparations. The party was small, composed of the group that had missed Hans's first reading: her husband, Herwarth Walden (originally Levin), and the painters Zech, Meidner, and Franz Marc.

The theme was Red. Zech dressed as the Devil. Marc wore a red horse's head. Wilhelm had had Reinhardt's costume shop cover him with arm-sized streamers of red satin, and had come as Blood. Paul had come as the Red Knight, his armor painted cardboard. Lasker-Schüler was all in blue.

Marc and Meidner immediately took to renovating everyone's costumes, pushing three tables together as their workspace; Marc in particular was so full of energy that Lasker-Schüler seemed chary and withdrawn by comparison. Paul went from being the Red Knight to the Red Cubist. Zech became the Scarlet Gryphon.

Wilhelm became the Deadly South Seas Carnivorous Underwater Plant.

Marc decided he was fascinated with Hans, whom he called An Animal of the Higher Hillsides. Marc was a Bavarian just back from Paris, and presented himself as an unstable mixture of bumpkin and expatriate. While Paul sat on Hans's shoulders, Paul's new cubist costume slowly falling apart, the three of them played a nonsensical rhyming game of Marc's invention. Wilhelm found himself in a seminar with Meidner, who'd been very excited by the recent production of *The Miracle*. Meidner vaporized about rhythm, dynamics, agitation, ecstasy, and motoricity. Wilhelm caught Hans's eye while the painter mopped his face, and mouthed, "Motoricity?"

When Meidner finally staggered off to relieve himself, Wilhelm sought out Walden, who was sitting by himself. He was pale, owlish, and not what they'd imagined as Lasker-Schüler's husband. He watched his wife across the room and alternated between parodying her hyperbole and offering more of his own. His wife dragged her family everywhere around the city, he said bitterly, and the best he could do was to take advantage of the situation by promoting his gallery and artists before the evening ended with his cuckolding in some other room of the house.

Wilhelm had no response.

"Go on, get out of here," Walden said, and Wilhelm left him alone.

Meidner as he said his goodbyes announced that he intended to paint Wilhelm's portrait and to portray him in a straw hat. Marc executed in blue chalk on the hallway wall a mural-sized blue ox and scribbled under it, *In the Spirit of Hans Ehrenbaum-Degele*.

Sharing their enthusiasm for these new wild-men painters and their work became a new way for the two friends to be together. Through Marc and Meidner they met more lunatics: Pechstein, the "nature-boy," with his uncomplicated manners and obsession with nude bathing; Kirchner, the neurasthenic, who so consistently flew into a rage if asked about his family in the provinces that his friends always did, for sport; and Kubin, who interpreted the world as poison and breakdown, and who finally stopped answering his bell and responded to calls from the street with only a wave from his window. They were struck by the ecstatic nervousness of these young men's paintings, like strike-storms signaling the release of psychic pressure. Being in their studios was like gazing upon handwriting *in extremis.*

They became part of the group, and christened themselves The Pathetic Ones. Hans and Zech even began a newsletter called *The New Pathos.*

They learned more about posturing. They viewed new forms of self-destructiveness. They saw the way an artwork could create a new vibration in the soul; the way it could play an ignorant game with the ultimate and still manage to evoke its own outline.

THE URGENCY of their sexual focus on one another came and went. They conducted themselves as if, even late at night, they were still on display. They had a saying for it whenever they lingered too long in each other's proximity: "The drapes are open."

Their intimacy was based instead on talk about sex. They slumped on their Oriental divan working themselves into a quiet agitation that would thrum through them all night. They talked about the pitfalls of physicality, and how it circumvented reason. The ideal was "friendship love," which didn't bear the mark of greed or thoughtless gratification, but instead focused on the willingness to sacrifice and the well-being of the other.

They pursued such insights sitting side by side, with their hands in their pockets.

Their rhetoric came from the Society of Free Spirits, an offshoot of Hirschfeld's Scientific-Humanitarian Committee, founded in opposition to §175, the statute against Contrary Sexual Sensibility. But while Hirschfeld had been convinced that science, combined with the necessary public education, would lead to the repeal—*Per scientia ad justiam*—the Society had put its trust in strong individuals who measured life's worth according to their own rules, free spirits who leaped all barriers and lived by their own authority, their goal the creation of a male culture. They would make no effort to generate pity, since that was an unmanly way of attempting to lift the criminal code.

Hans and Wilhelm had joined, though they kept their distance and only occasionally attended round tables on the creation of a lasting and noble society.

Still, they lived under the shadow of §175. Repeal was impossible. Who would even sign the petitions? A few years earlier, one of the Kaiser's closest friends had been toppled by just the insinuation in a magazine that he deviated from the norm in psychic-sexual terms.

They subscribed to Hirschfeld's *Yearbook for Intermediate Sexual Tendencies*. In the front were scholarly articles. In the back were press reports of convictions under §175, as well as for blackmail. The obituary page had a special subsection for suicides.


CHRISTMAS WAS approaching. They suffered through four straight days of freezing rain. It occurred to them that they still hadn't gone on that long voyage they'd promised themselves. They still couldn't afford to. But in the hope of rededicating themselves to each other, they decided that a weekend trip to the south might do. At one of the society's gatherings they'd met a young man whose mother ran a ski lodge in Murnau, a spa village in Bavaria. The lodge was near a waterfall and superb hiking trails. It was also of the sort Berliners called storm-free: where your hosts asked no questions and refused to be shocked by anything.

Outwardly they treated the trip as they had any of their other excursions. Inwardly it was as though their hearts were diving-bells, constricting and expanding from the changes in pressure.

Long stretches of the trip made no impression on their memories. A snowy hillside outside Augsburg. A black dog up to his chin in snow. Hans losing a glove in the taxi to the lodge. They barely spoke, and were unable to read. In their room the night they arrived, they ate smoked ham, cheese, black bread with mustard, grapes, and chocolate cake. They warmed Hans's hand before the fire.

They bathed and sat before the hearth buried under thick rugs. It was puzzling, Hans ventured, that physical pleasures, precarious at best and rare, were regarded with such mistrust by the so-called wise. Could they think of any happier couples, among those they knew? They spent all their time denouncing the dangers of sensual excess instead of fearing its absence or loss, while the energy they put into tyrannizing their senses could be better spent embellishing their souls.

They kissed, each of them shaking.

Hans rose to rummage through his rucksack. Shivering, he returned to their rugs. He had a page marked in his copy of Xenophon. He opened to it and read: *"Xenophon had with him an Olynthian called Episthenes, who on this occasion saw a good-looking boy at the most beautiful age, on the point of being put to death; so he ran to Xenophon and begged him to intercede. Xenophon went to Seuthes and asked him not to kill the boy. Seuthes said: And would you, Episthenes, be willing to die for the boy? Episthenes stretched out his neck and said: Strike the blow if the boy tells you to. Seuthes then asked the boy whom he should kill. The boy said: Kill me. And at this Episthenes put his arms around the boy and said: Now you will have to fight me for him. For I shall never give him up.*

*"And Seuthes laughed, and let the matter rest."*

And still they did nothing! They lay, heads together, watching the fire in a state of such excitement that when fatigue hit, it struck them all at once.

Wilhelm woke with the fire diminished, and the room dark. He dragged himself to his feet and whispered for Hans to come to bed. Hans followed him under the fat comforters, and they fell asleep.

Plumpe asleep: the circulation of his blood, his measured breathing, the delicate function of his kidneys, the world of dreams in his head—all linked to the power of fate.

Hans woke him. The fire was out. The winter outside howled through the darkness. The lodge's welcoming bell clinked under its ice sheath.

His hand on Wilhelm's belly moved to his sex, cupping it as it grew. His fingers encircled and pulled, as if drawing out the erection. He quoted Xenophon again, to give Wilhelm courage. *"All these soldiers have their eyes on you,"* he whispered, lowering his face to Wilhelm's hip. *"If they see that you're downhearted, they'll become cowards; while if you are yourself prepared, they will follow."*

He held Wilhelm still, as if pondering something. For Wilhelm it was a thrilling moment of privacy violated, as if his life had taken a leap that made everything more worthwhile. Poor Spiess, he thought, feeling his happiness rise; poor Veidt; poor Else.

"My Wilhelm," Hans whispered. "My cold boy of understanding." He put Wilhelm to his lips. Wilhelm gave himself over, wanting to let himself be taught, and to let himself teach. A phrase of schoolboy Apollonius streamed through him: ψυχὴ γὰρ νεφέεσσι μεταχρονίη πεπότητο ("For her psyche had taken flight high among the clouds"). Hans lifted him off the bed with his hands and his mouth, and eased him back down.

In such a situation, Wilhelm dreamed. He dreamed he was free and that people loved him. He'd done nothing wrong and was fully happy, and the one he loved most was kissing him. He felt that unsettlement at his heart, that absolute stripping down. What he learned, shockingly vivid, dimmed immediately, as illness does for convalescents. It was a glimpse into that other world.

He slept. In the moments before he woke, he savored his existence as someone else, without future or past.

THE NEXT morning, when he emerged dazed and dripping from a bath, Hans had arranged before them on their dressing table an English breakfast: strong red tea from a teapot Wilhelm could hardly lift, with jam, scones, bacon and eggs, oatcakes, potted meat, and home-baked bread.

He was changing his name, Wilhelm announced. It was the first thing he'd said that morning. He was no longer Wilhelm Plumpe. From that moment on, he was Friedrich Wilhelm Murnau. He was breaking with one family to better signal his allegiance to another.

HANS WAS unusually silent the rest of the day. In the lodge's parlor the next morning, as they were making ready to leave, he presented Wilhelm with his schoolboy's copy of *Faust*. On the inside cover, he'd inscribed, *To Murnau. Christmas, 1910.* Even then, even there, out of deference to the other lodgers, they refrained from a prolonged embrace.

# VERDUN,
# 1917

FOUR MONTHS after the war began, Murnau was called up into the First Regiment of the Foot Guards at Potsdam, perhaps because of his size. Hans had volunteered with a less elite unit the month before.

Two weeks before reporting, Hans had gone with his family on a ski vacation. Murnau had been unable to go, due to a rehearsal schedule, so he sat around the Romanische feeling neglected and sorry for himself. Even Lasker-Schüler had left Berlin, on a lecture tour.

Unable to sleep, he walked the streets. Prowling the park one night, he was reunited with Spiess, who had been in the company of a young sailor. The sailor seemed mortified by their encounter. Spiess and Murnau exchanged addresses, and Spiess again proclaimed his old friend's change of name a great amusement. The next day, he sent round to Murnau's house a dozen chocolate roses and a ticket to the Philharmonic.

At dinner that night Murnau felt taken up by more capable hands. It was decided that he should improve his English. The merits of different teachers were discussed. None were apparently satisfactory on the issue of pronunciation. And naturally, given the political situation, finding a young Englishman was out of the question. Every so often the entire clientele of the restaurant broke out in patriotic songs.

After dinner they returned to Spiess's apartment near the Oranienburger Tor, tucked in the back of a Period house. The inner door shut out the noise of the war demonstrations. Spiess went around the room lighting candles while Murnau studied the familiar antique bronze screen for the fireplace and the small silver casket suspended above the bed. The landscapes with their trees and broken figures were still visible down the hall in a studio. The rooms looked much as they had seven years earlier: somewhere between ransacked and rearranged, as though Gypsies had spent the weekend.

Spiess presented some of his experiments relating to his theory of colors. The theory was new to Murnau, and stupid. Sitting in little wooden armchairs, they talked about Murnau's most recent roles. Spiess was flatteringly detailed in his comments. About criticism in general, he claimed that through the daily reviews a sort of half-culture found its way to the masses, but to productive talent, that same criticism was a noxious mist.

They talked for four hours and in the middle of the night found themselves asleep on the same sofa.

The candles were out. Spiess began easing off Murnau's shoes, rocking each heel gently free.

He brought his face close. He smelled like candlewicks. Murnau held his breath. Spiess licked his finger and glossed it gently over Murnau's lips and back across his gums. He leaned in to Murnau's ear and whispered something about a priestly rite.

"This is demonic," Murnau murmured.

Spiess was already undressed. He said quietly that the more elevated a man was, the more he was influenced by demons.

Murnau didn't tell him to stop. He'd always assumed that a certain feeling for beauty would serve him in place of virtue, and render him immune to the coarser solicitations. But he lay there in the dark enjoying what was happening, reminded of Medea with Jason: shame holding her still while shameless desire urged her on. Spiess freed him from his clothes as if unwrapping glassware.

Murnau left while it was still dark. He stood outside Spiess's apartment in the frigid blue light, matting his hair down and smelling his hands. Someone's milk delivery had shattered on the stoop because of the cold. He thought, *The frivolous finds eloquence in relation to the important because of what it debases and destroys.*

THE NEXT morning, Spiess met Hans on the way to Murnau's apartment. Murnau heard them laughing as they came up the stairs. Spiess was saying, "Now where do we meet an original nature? Where's the man who has the strength to be true, to show himself as he is?" as Murnau opened the door.

They said their hellos, and stood about in the entryway like spear-carriers who had forgotten their blocking. Hans had his hands in his armpits to warm them. "Today we celebrate the regeneration of the sun!" Spiess finally said, and crossed to the window and drew up the blinds. Hans, in mid-smile, saw Murnau's face and understood.

If Murnau could have forgiven himself for everything else, he could not have forgiven his responsibility for that moment. What they both understood was how inevitable the moment had been.

He watched Hans's contentment transformed into the damaged wariness of a child's understanding that his loved ones weren't motivated only by selflessness. Hans left the apartment and thumped back down the stairs.

HANS WAS billeted in various places, and it took him three months to answer Wilhelm's letters. When Spiess made a joke about the Foreign Legion, Murnau nearly struck him.

*We're not forced into our mistakes by the maneuverings of outside agents,* he wrote in his journal; *our vices are capable of generating fantastic illusions and idiocies all by themselves.*

To Hans he wrote about Lasker-Schüler, who had heard about his betrayal. He wrote about Marc, off at the front himself, and his insistence that the war was a clarion-call waking the sleeping and the lazy. He was still painting blue oxen, now on postcards.

When Hans didn't answer, he wrote of his own call-up. He wrote of heavy fighting, and being made an officer. He described the shattering noise of his unit's nightly artillery bombardments, and about mornings of feeling like a stranger pulling another stranger out of bed. He wrote about the kind of courage he wanted to possess: cool and detached, free from physical excitement. He hadn't achieved it, he wrote, though his bunk-mates believed that he had.

He wrote of becoming a company commander at Riga. He wrote about his envy for those in the Flying Corps. He asked if Hans remembered the exhibitions before the war when all those sportsmen turned in their Mercedes so they could kill themselves in the air instead.

He told Hans that he'd sent many more letters than Hans had received: unwritten, happy, sad, chatty, and fearful.

It wasn't until he quoted two lines from Rimbaud's *Une Saison en enfer*—*It will come, it will come / The time with which one can fall in love!*—that Hans answered.

He sent a packet. On top was a *Simplicissimus* cartoon called "Barbarian Girls," in which happy maidens pored over a map of London marked "Zeppelin Targets." One girl boasted, "And here our flyers will destroy St. Mark's Square with bombs," and another responded, "My God! The poor pigeons."

In a note beneath the cartoon Hans thanked him for his letters. He'd heard from Lasker-Schüler and Veidt, and both were well. Paul had been a steady correspondent. He thanked Murnau for his concern. He said there was no need to apologize or to castigate oneself. He asked if Murnau had written to his parents. He closed with a new poem:

> *The hours go slowly.*
> *Awake. Dig trenches and softly sing.*
> *Dream of country; of happiness and going home.*
> *Patience becomes duty. Waiting becomes action.*
> *Across the German earth, the claxon of bells.*

*The snow of a dreary winter coats the shoulder,*
*layers the moth-eaten cap.*

At the bottom of the packet, he'd wrapped some chocolate. On the wrapping he'd written: *Saved this for you.*

MURNAU HEARD nothing again for a month. He was lounging in his dugout, his back to a quilt he'd hung for insulation, reading a months-old magazine by candlelight, when he was handed a dispatch. He was too bored to read it. Eventually he finished his leafing around and picked it up. Some kind of lorry-load could be heard roiling past in the mud outside. The dispatch read: *Hans Ehrenbaum was killed in action in Russia on July 28th.* It was from his commanding officer, whom Hans had asked to notify Murnau in the event of his death. The other lounging lieutenant left the dugout when he realized Murnau had received bad news. That day Murnau's company was standing down, waiting to be resupplied. He was temporarily relieved of his duties. He remained in the dugout.

How had it happened? Were they sure he was dead? He called through to Hans's unit from the captain's field telephone. The voice on the other end said that they'd identified his torso. He'd been given a field burial.

Murnau returned to his dugout. He cracked his head going down the steps.

Ideas jarred one upon the other. Over the course of the afternoon, fellow officers dropped in to offer condolences. Words ground on. His jaw felt dislocated. His hands were filthy with mud from the floor.

In hospitals, he'd seen men beat their heads against the wall in grief. On pickets, he'd seen a guard dog refuse to eat or sleep because its companion animal had been killed. He cried his way into coughing fits.

He sat on the dugout floor, stripped of the physical strength he needed for work.

What about Hans's mother? he thought. The notion was a flare that burned away self-pity.

His captain came by. Murnau thanked him for letting him telephone. The captain waved it off. He borrowed Murnau's candle, saying he needed more light to catch someone cheating at skat.

It grew dark outside. A short rain came and went.

Starlight made pale gleams on the runoff through the doorway.

He was buried alive by the news.

It was an easy declension to work out. Hans had been killed in Russia. Hans had been killed in Russia because he'd served in the Fusiliers. Hans had been where he'd been with the Fusiliers because of when he'd volunteered. And Hans had volunteered when he had because of Murnau.


THE NEXT day he resumed his duties. A legend grew up around his reception of the news. It was repeated to the new men, at times when Murnau was within earshot. According to the story, he'd been in his dugout when the message came. Practicing the stoicism he preached, he'd read the dispatch twice, nodded in private meditation, folded it into a pocket, and then had busied himself at his work, saying nothing about it to anyone, then or afterwards. He was supposed to have responded to the captain's consolatory visit with the comment "My friend still lives as our model."

Both his fellow lieutenant from the dugout and the captain allowed the story to circulate, he assumed because of its inspirational value.

. . .

HE WANTED to write his father and tell him that his son had finally become everyone's model Prussian.


BY SEPTEMBER he began petitioning for transfer to the Flying Corps.


THE DECISION would take months. In the meantime his unit held a stalemated part of the line.

In October, Herr Ehrenbaum died. Murnau received a note from Mary Degele.

In November, he was able to visit her on a three-day leave.

She came out onto the front walk to greet him. Inside, they hung on each other and sobbed like children. She fed him some sausage and then they fell asleep, exhausted.

He awoke with her at his bedside. They spoke as if he were the one convalescing. She had recently had a visit from Lasker-Schüler, who was currently obsessed with a Pole named von Twardowski. Paul seemed inconsolable, devastated by the news about Hans.

She'd received condolence letters from everyone. Some from boys Murnau knew: Conrad Veidt; that other boy with the weight problem; Walter Spiess from that Baltic family.

They shared a pot of tea and some fruit. She sat Indian-style on the bed. The lines of her throat were still beautiful. Her eyes seemed to be fighting against smoke. She worried about Lasker-Schüler's plans for a memorial evening, and hoped he would have a talk with the woman. The New Youth Group was helping to fund it.

She worried about his health. She urged him to try to transfer to civil duty.

He asked after her health. Her heart difficulties had started up again.

She said that she hoped he would come live with her, after the war. She said that it was what Hans would have wanted.

The offer set him off on a weeping fit despite himself. She waited and then let herself out.

Around dawn, she came back to his bedroom, and lay down beside him. He kissed her. She was crying. He held her in his arms. They were unable to speak, but together under the covers, they fell back to sleep.

When they woke, they lay together like lovers. She asked how he went on. He told her that ambition was at least something; and that he now lived animalistically and had shut off everything spiritual. She said she was sure that wasn't true.

At the end of his leave he tucked her in for a nap. She was too demoralized by his leaving to see him off. In his last few minutes in the house, he stripped, and then remade, the bed in Hans's room.

Before he left her, he was only able to say, "This was all my fault." She shushed him, crying. She kissed him again. He left the house. Back out on the street, he murmured, *Dixi et salvi animam meam.* I have spoken and saved my soul. But he hadn't.

THE MEMORIAL evening came off six months later, at the Secession Hall in Charlottenburg. In the meantime he'd been granted his petition to join the Air Force. He arranged his transfer to coincide with the memorial, which turned out to be dedicated to two poets, Hans and Georg Trakl, a suicide. Lasker-Schüler delivered the eulogy, which he found disappointing. Afterwards Hans's publisher talked to him about bringing out a new edition of the poems now, rather than waiting until the end of the war, since it was clear the war would never end.

.  .  .

A FEW weeks after leaving Mary Degele, he had seen his first military airplane, a Fokker Eindekker. The prewar flying machines, once considered so wondrous, were by that point everyday transportation. Mechanics drifted back and forth, bored, while the Fokkers' engines turned over. He stood transfixed, as if by the noise and power of a hundred lions. This was good news, since what he needed most of all was to rediscover the possibility of joy. Joy was the equivalent of strength. Men who lived without it were corpses.

The required medical tests were less than severe, due to the mounting casualty rate among pilots and observers. So lenient was the medical establishment in its quest for bodies that during his eye test at Halberstadt, his examiner said, "The second line, third letter: I see a 'B.' What do you see?"

His early training was a similar joke. The technique was that of governesses teaching toddlers to swim. The novices perched in the noses of old Taubes while the instructors ran up the engines and shouted incomprehensible things into the slipstream.

The Taubes had dual controls. Verbal instructions were impossible. The pupil rested his hands and feet on the joystick and rudder bars, as if palpating a sunburn, while the instructor flew. The theory was to allow the pupil to feel the instructor's instincts.

Eventually, if they hadn't killed themselves, they were shipped as flying pupils to the Aviation Replacement Section at Johannisthal. There they trained in LVG two-seaters.

Wherever he went, his peers found him hard to get along with. He was a fastidious introvert. His attitudes toward women seemed puritanical. He spent his off-duty hours with his correspondence.

But his grief refused to dissipate, and flooded everything. What he responded to in flying was the way that all that was important and distinctive on the ground was of no consequence to the aviator. The aviator soared above the catastrophe, his eyes elsewhere.

Murnau soloed after fifty-four dual flights, and nine days later passed his preliminary certification. He was moved to replacement section Number 2, at Adlershof, for advanced training. There he survived a minor crash. For his final tests, he made two flights to Döberitz and a long cross-country flight. He graduated in early February and awaited orders. He began active service a week later at Rethel, flying mail and spare parts to the front.

HE WAS assigned to an observation squadron based near Tellancourt that flew Aviatiks. They were quartered in a beautiful and disintegrating château abandoned by its owners. It was the dead of winter. He was given one of the smallest rooms in the back, with a faulty stove. He flew across the lines every day the weather allowed, then moved on to artillery spotting.

After cocoa and biscuits at 4:30 a.m., he climbed into his flying suit with Hans a part of his thoughts each bitterly cold morning. Once he and his observer finished dressing, they were bundled like bears in fur, their faces below their goggles greased for protection against the wind. The airfield was a cinder runway cut through acres of beet and kale.

When the engine turned over, warm oil misted back and they were constantly wiping their goggles. With any sideslips, great blasts of air buffeted around the windscreen. At altitude they occasionally found themselves in the trajectories of the big shells. The plane rocked like a canoe whenever one went by. Their anti-aircraft fire used black cordite, which lingered after the fighting had passed over. Traversing a belt of it during a calm stretch produced an uneasiness he couldn't locate until later, when he smelled his flying clothes.

At six thousand meters, the entire western front from the Alps to the North Sea was visible. They had the sky to themselves.

Where were the French planes? They didn't know. They studied the great Boelcke's discourse on the techniques of air fighting. After his death, the order had been given that every airman should be able to repeat it verbatim. At the funeral it was said that Richthofen himself had pledged, "I will be a Boelcke."

They were not Boelckes. They knew only a few things.

Murnau's first enemy plane was a light blue Caudron, lumbering along against the wind. He and his observer came across it when straggling back alone after a cannister-drop. It looked like a flying wire entanglement. They approached to within a hundred yards and did nothing, staring at the two miniature humans in their French birdcage. Why kill them? Why even shoot at them?

The French observer suffered no such inhibitions, and splintered Murnau's observer's goggles. After they landed, the observer was carried off to a field hospital and never seen again.

The French fighters arrived soon afterwards. Murnau came to realize that the reconnaissance pilot who survived six weeks was blessed with rare ability and luck. At altitude he enjoyed the illusion he was moving at a respectable pace until some Frenchman came speeding at him in a Nieuport. At that point he was the cornered stag; he sweated, panic kicked at his stomach, and he could only stay his easterly course home and summon every trick he knew to shun the fusillade of bullets. Each time, he had no idea how he survived. Sometimes the attacker was exceptionally unskilled or else his fuel ran low, or his guns jammed, or his ammunition gave out. Sometimes, after they rolled to a stop back at the airfield, their machine shot to pieces, he had no explanation.

And combat maneuvering was more dangerous than enemy bullets: simple banks sheared away wing struts or tore out stay wires at their roots. He watched a friend's machine during one maneuver break up in the sky as if dispersing into its component parts.

He put in for transfer to a fighter squadron. In his petition, he pointed out that he'd bring to his new task a special cunning. The former reconnaissance pilot understood his victims' plight, and could anticipate their thinking. It was no coincidence that so many aces were ex-reconnaissance men, since only the fittest had lived to pilot single-seaters in the first place.

In the meantime his unit tried every formation: the line, the echelon, the vee. One observer carried a carbine with a gramophone nailed to the stock in the hopes of terrifying the enemy. In their mess they collected the sheared propeller blades from their own wrecks. They carved the walnut and mahogany into tobacco jars or mounts for clocks. Observers got the shivering fits, and there was a great deal of drunkenness. A pilot was found outside the mechanics' quarters before dawn, drunkenly shouting, "Give me an airplane! I can't stay on this earth any longer!"

AND YET when his transfer came through and he was asked by his commanding officer if he was ready to fly alone, he wanted to answer, "I'm too afraid." But standing there, he swallowed one kind of cowardice so that he could avoid another.

HE WAS assigned to Jagdstaffel 4, outside Sivry. He'd be flying an Albatros D of a very advanced design. The fuselage was of semi-monocoque construction covered in plywood instead of fabric, for reinforced strength. It had a shark's profile. It was outfitted with a 160-horsepower water-cooled Mercedes engine. He took it up for some trial spins and was exhilarated.

Everyone had started to paint their machines in individual ways. Murnau had his finished a midnight blue, top and bottom. The Jasta symbol on the fuselage was a fanged serpent. Behind it he had painted *H. E.-D.*

Verdun was eight kilometers to the south. From the air he could see the emplacements for the twelve-inch naval cannon and the 420mm siege mortars imported the year before for the great battle. They stretched on for thirty miles.

The day he arrived, he met Allmenröder squelching around in the frozen mud directing the unpacking of a new aircraft. He'd come to aviation from the cavalry, the Second Westphalian(!) Hussars with whom he'd seen action in the east. His unit had once counterattacked with Hans's Fusiliers. He'd also started in an Aviatik. He had deep-set eyes and a sad, tremulous expression when he joked. He considered his most prominent feature to be his ears, which he kept tucked under his flying-cap. He'd lately celebrated his twentieth birthday. When Murnau met him, he already had two kills.

He was another loner, forever tinkering with his machine. He'd flown in the Battle of the Somme and every single man he'd begun with had since been killed. In his room he had as a single decoration a page torn from a book of Persian miniatures. The page featured warrior companions.

They became a world unto themselves. What they enjoyed was not so much intimacy as shared isolation. Their mates gave them a wide berth. For a week their Jasta huddled around stoves while freezing rain poured down. The hangars sprang great leaks.

They talked about flying. Because Allmenröder had also flown a two-seater, he referred to those crews as Poor Devils, and always aimed only to down the machine. He also fiddled with inventions. He showed Murnau the new gunsight he'd constructed to his own specifications: two concentric circles etched on a lens, their diameters covering one meter and ten meters at a distance of a hundred meters. Thus when he had sighted on an airplane and knew the wingspan or fuselage length, he could precisely evaluate range and judge the moment to fire.

Since Murnau was nine years older, Allmenröder called him Grandfather, and began schooling Grandfather in the hopes of keeping him alive. He demanded knowledge of the machine, tired of young cavalry officers who knew nothing about the internal combustion engine; they went off on long screaming pursuit dives and in the process allowed revolutions to build to the point of engine failure. Try talking to some of those Hussars about oil temperature or compression ratios or valve overlap! They thought such matters were best left to the troops, meaning their mechanics, whom they treated like grooms.

He showed Murnau why tactical skills were composed of many things: awareness of clouds and wind, nerves and reaction speed, sensitivity to the aircraft. And vision, as a function of experience and intuition—a manner of focusing that allowed aircrews to notice the minute and menacing details on which everything depended.

Talking with Allmenröder, he began to understand flight itself as a new manner of perception: whereas the old way had been to look from a stationary point at objects before you, here you moved *through* and swept *across* the image. The act of taking aim was itself a geometrification of seeing, by technically aligning ocular perception along an imaginary axis. The French called it *ligne de foi*—the faith line. What sort of image could the photographer record with such an advantage? What sort of image could a *motion picture* record?

When the weather let up, they took off in the pre-dawn murk for patrols over enemy territory. Allmenröder stuffed his pockets with cake, which he ate aloft by the handfuls. On sunset patrols, Allmenröder and Murnau were always the last to land.

While everyone else was safe on the ground, they climbed to six thousand meters above their airfield to view the spectacle. The russet and violet spread in great streams across the sky, north, south, east, and west. Thousands of square miles of cloud plain were luminous with the setting sun. No explorer of the Poles had seen such a breathtaking and unbroken expanse. It was Reinhardt's *Kuppelhorizont*. Allmenröder and Murnau in their rackety little machines saw and touched that kind of happiness. Murnau thought, We're not only actors in a bloody conflict; we're also the first spectators of this magic, pyrotechnic fairy-play.

Eventually he told Allmenröder about Hans's death. Allmenröder had assumed something of that sort. He'd had a special friend, too, whom he could not bring himself to name.

They began to notice on their patrols a few lone aircraft who kept an eye on them but turned and ran if approached. They had names for them, based on their markings: Skull and Crossbones, or Blue Fin, or Yellow Wheels. They had particular affection for a clumsy two-seater they called the Flying Pig. Its crew was so incompetent that they refrained from shooting at it. Frightening the crew was, however, considered fair sport. Whenever approached, the poor Frenchmen began a series of spastic turns and maneuvers, opening fire from absurdly long range.

On leave in Cologne, they had a card made at a printer's that they could hand out when cornered:

*PLEASE!!!*
*Do not ask us anything about flying.*
*You will find the usual queries answered below:*
*1. Yes, we are part of a pursuit squadron.*
*2. Sometimes it's dangerous, sometimes it's not.*
*3. The higher we fly, the colder it is.*
*4. We notice that by freezing when it's colder.*
*5. Flying height, 2000–7000 meters.*
*6. Yes, we can see things at that height, though not so well.*
*7. We can't see through a telescope because it shakes.*
*8. Yes, we've dropped bombs.*
*9. Yes, we've downed enemy aircraft.*
*10. Yes, we've seen the loss of many friends.*

In early April on a sunset patrol, seven Nieuports howled down at them from out of a cloudbank. They had no chance to outrun them. On the first pass, tracers speared out in all directions, and everyone broke up or down, right or left, whipping around to bring guns to bear. He lost track of Allmenröder. No one held a straight course or steady bank for more than a second.

His ears grew accustomed to such noise that he ceased to hear it; he flew in a deafening silence.

He was singled out for special attention by a silver aircraft with a black bat behind its roundel on the fuselage. They chased each other's tails, losing height, whirling like the cups of an anemometer, their wings banked almost all the way over, craning their necks at each other across a diameter of a few hundred feet.

Finally, with his superior horsepower, Murnau closed the circle. They continued to turn in a near-vertical bank. Each time, the Frenchman's skill in throttling back allowed his craft to sideslip out of the gunsight. With each turn they lost altitude. Finally they soared between two tall trees. The Frenchman had nowhere to go. He pulled back completely on his stick. His lower wings sheared off and his Nieuport folded and tumbled forward end over end into the roof of a barn. Murnau flew through the explosion and a piece of debris holed his upper wing.

The sky around him was empty as he ascended, the fighting having moved off in another direction. There was cloud cover to the west.

He flew home alone, watching for pursuit. One hand was shaking. He didn't know how to feel. It was as though a boy with whom he'd been playing had killed himself on a dare.

He was washed and dressed when Allmenröder finally straggled in, delighted to hear about his success. That evening at mess he toasted Murnau and two others who'd scored victories.

The French pilots, he reported with annoyance, had singled him out for combat even before some of the greenhorns. The next day, he had his mechanic paint across his top wing *Have You Forgotten Me?*

THEY FLEW more patrols. Without reinforcements, it was only a matter of time. Things came apart very quickly. One morning they lost three fledglings in a single swoop. Murnau had his tail shot off and crashed into a shallow stream. He rode back to the aerodrome in the back of a truck, the driver taking the turns at top speed while he looked out at the fog and black sky. The mist was broken from time to time by the flashing of the guns.

Pilots began turning back from sorties. Their commanding officer was brought down into a stand of young birches so that the joystick dislocated his jaw and perforated his palate. On the third sortie of a cold and rainy day, Allmenröder broke left into a purple rain cloud while Murnau broke right, tracers spiraling past their wings, and Murnau never saw him again.

HE WAS disciplined after subsequent flights for continuing the search on his own, and was grounded as a disciplinary measure. Had they not been in such desperate need of experienced pilots, he would have been sacked.

There was a service. Murnau was asked to speak. When his turn came, he said only that it was as if the heavens hadn't consented to return his friend to earth. Afterwards he was told that he'd been inspirational. His response initiated another disciplinary proceeding.

His Jasta was thrown into the attempt to stop a minor ground-offensive east of Verdun. Asked to fly protection flights and infantry-contact patrols, which meant essentially ground attack, he did so day after day without rest. No fancy acrobatics or stunt flying. Destruction was the goal.

The French troops were butchered. They hid from him the way the moles he caught as a boy and tossed into his garden disappeared, as if into water. While he machine-gunned, he continued to consider this new way of seeing. In his journal he wrote, *I am an icy scientist, and for me their war is a laboratory experiment.*

He crashed again, and again walked away from it. He pinwheeled around a willow and ended on his head in a pile of sugar beets, branches and struts all around him. The control stick had ruptured his kidney.

He was back from the field hospital in four weeks, no longer passing blood. But urination involved doubling over in pain.

The aviators of Jagdstaffel 4 put on a New Year's variety show. Participation was compulsory. Either because he was such an outsider or because they knew of his theatrical background, the officers of the mess listed him last on the program. He stayed in his quarters until summoned. The emcee introduced him as "That mixture of wandering Gypsy, total misanthrope, and cultivated gentleman, our own grandfather of the theater, Herr Lieutenant Dr. Murnau."

He went around the room extinguishing candles, leaving only the light from the fireplace. Then he mounted the platform. He recited "The Pianist of Death." The fire painted the young faces of his audience. He gave the poem a strange intonation, half pathetic and half sinister. His audience was captivated. Officers drummed their fingers in time to the *trum trum trum* of the refrain.

Outside it was dark and cold. For the poem's final line he drew himself to his full height, stretched his arm toward the airfield, and cried, *"There, on that bier, / Behold the last of my sons!"*

There was a storm of applause. He was shoved and pulled back up to the platform for an encore. With tears in his eyes and his back to his comrades, he recited "Three Old Troopers, Round the Hearth of Heaven."

He was assured afterwards that he'd never been more a part of the Jasta. The next day he made firm his resolution to desert. He would fly to Switzerland, crash his machine, and absent himself from this war.

ON THE appointed morning, he remarked to the squadron blab-bermouth before run-up that he was having trouble with his compass. Upon take-off, with his Jasta he headed west, and like his friend Allmenröder, he pitched into a cloud and was never seen again. He flew south-southeast, headed for Andermatt. He was over Switzerland in a matter of hours, flying over lofty woodlands and deep vaporous valleys.

He descended through veils of mist. Moisture hung in the air. In some valleys lines of hedges bordered fields. He picked out a gentle downward slope at the end of which was a thicket. He brought in the Albatros with a calculated excess of speed, and bounced it along the snow until the thicket tore off its bottom wing.

He switched off the engine. It sputtered and stopped. Nearby, he could hear a cowbell. The engine ticked and pinged as it cooled. He unfastened his seat harness and climbed from the cockpit.

The snow crunched underfoot. To the south, he could see cleared fields and a village. Crows were cawing somewhere.

Art's many paths lay before him, unrestricted. He had to make up his mind, had to focus his ambition, in order to achieve peace and quiet in his sleep. He had to choose and stick to a path. He had to be hard. He had to hoard his sorrow. Existence would have more to teach, and he'd listen to its secret instructions.

The war was drinking the blood of millions. Allmenröder was gone. Hans was gone. The war had taken his partner in sadness and, before that, his lover. What warmth he experienced from their memory felt like the last efforts of a solitary, struggling against the closing of the box.

But he had his work, whatever it would be. Already he could no longer *think* what he liked; moving images substituted themselves for his thoughts. His experience in the Air Corps had exploded his old homogeneity of vision. From that day onward, he would be free of human immobility. He would be in perpetual movement. He would approach and draw away from things—rising up as if with aircraft—to fall and fly at one with bodies falling and rising through the air. He would re-create those moments of extraordinary power: the freeze of the dive-wind on their faces; the constant swallowing, at altitude, to stop the deafness; the smell of the varnish; the moonlight shining in their struts; the stars between their wings.

# BERLIN,
# 1921

HE WAS up all night. He imagined the wind making weather-vane soup for the insomniacs. He was sitting at his desk in his study. There was a breeze. The night air filled the room.

Hans was the anguish that pulled its plow through his sleep. After six years, Murnau was still a house in which the largest room was sealed.

On nights like that he sorted through involuntary memories with a narcissist's absorption. Mary Degele had claimed that in the old days on stormy spring nights, they could breathe the fresh sea air, blown all the way in to the city from the North Sea.

One night years ago, a man had set up a telescope on the main street in Wilhelmshöhe, asking twenty pfennigs a look. Twenty pfennigs to infinity! Fourteen-year-old Wilhelm had had the twenty pfennigs. The moon had swum in the dark lens-circle.

During Murnau's flirtation with Veidt, Hans had sent him a cautionary parable printed on a stiff card: *Unable to resist, a boy took a bite from a gingerbread heart he'd intended for his sweetheart. To restore its original shape, he was forced to take more bites, and more, each time to no avail, forming his gingerbread successively into a circle, a square, a smaller and smaller heart.*

Under some preliminary correspondence concerning locations, he found a buttered roll on its little dish. Somewhere along the line, he'd evolved into a man of strong opinions and solitary meals.

Under the roll was his typed response to *Film-Kurier*'s request, for their Christmas issue, for an autobiography and "dream-list for a cinema of the future." He was unhappy with the false jauntiness of what he had so far:

*F. W. Murnau, thirty-two years old, sighs like Alexander for more worlds to conquer. He rose from spear-carrier for Max Reinhardt to filmmaking in ten years. He first appeared in the Deutsches Theater in '09, having won a scholarship after Reinhardt had seen him in an amateur production. He remained in the company until conscripted, working as assistant director whenever possible.*

*As far as can be discovered, he has looked thirty-five and has been six foot four ever since he was twelve. Under Reinhardt his first roles paid three marks a week. His first star turn involved a battle-axe and a fantastic headpiece that obscured his face. Realizing there was little call for giants onstage, he threw in his lot with motion pictures. Since then he's been secretary, travel agent, still photographer, publicity writer, film cutter, title writer, handholder, and actor; everything but the night watchman. He began attracting attention by knocking over sets, volunteering for jobs for which he was hopelessly unqualified, and generally treating the serious side of studio life with unconscious humor. He was fired periodically and always reported again the next morning. Soon it became clear that since he had no usefulness in any single area of filmmaking, he had better become the boss, and direct. All the honors heaped upon him since then would form a very small pile.*

*And with all respect to Father Christmas, Murnau hasn't any Utopian wishes to request; he has given up hoping for the perfect script, or the international star who doesn't aim at being one, or the permanent company of actors at his disposal. But although such presents are beyond the bounds of possibility, Father Christmas' magic wand could create the instrument which is much more important: the camera that can move freely in space.*

*What Murnau dreams of, when he lays his sleepless head to its pillow at night, is the camera that at any moment can go anywhere, at any speed. The camera that outstrips present film technique and fulfills the cinema's ultimate artistic goal. The first difference between cinema and photography has to be that the viewpoint can be mobile, can share the speed of moving objects. He wants, viewed through mobile space, the encounter of surfaces; stimulation and its opposite, calm; a symphony made of the harmony of bodies and the rhythm of space; the play of pure movement, vigorous and abundant. He wants new modes of expression corresponding to the art of the image-machine, and he seeks them with the utmost perseverance. He wants the camera to be both participant and observer, like the dreamer who acts and watches himself doing so. He wants to move from the geometry of the one-dimensional surface to the geometry that applies in depth.*

*He wants to rid motion pictures of what does not belong to them, all that is unnecessary and trivial and drawn from other sources. That is what will be accomplished when films reach the level of art.*

*Here then, Father Christmas, is Murnau's dream: he is in an unimaginably modern theater, gazing spellbound at an immense screen. He sees projected a film by an unknown filmmaker that is awesomely beautiful, inconceivable, and totally unfamiliar. He cannot even imagine how it was composed. He's not even sure he's watching a film. He sees, illuminated there, the simplest and most elusive of miracles: the path to himself and his neighbors.*

Mary Degele's old gardens were still dark. He had not maintained her fastidiousness about keeping after the gardener after her death. The trees emanated a calm, pre-dawn hush. Two clouds hung above them.

He turned on his lamp. His kidneys felt swollen. He wrote himself a note: *Be sure of having used to the full all that's communicated by immobility and silence.*

He pulled over *The History of Witchcraft* and opened to the chapter on vampires. The house was quiet. He paged through engravings. The *osculum infame,* the kiss of shame: witches kissing Satan's backside.

For two days he'd been squabbling with Spiess, who wanted to accompany them to Slovakia. He claimed he could be of service. And he could keep Murnau out of trouble. One thing that was very strong in him was fidelity, he said. Promiscuity, too, but also fidelity.

He wanted to go along on salary, Murnau supposed. Of course, Spiess said. He was doing so as an artist, not a companion. The argument had been suspended.

He shut *The History of Witchcraft.* Work on something, he thought.

He considered an idea for the shot of the spider that Knock would see from his madman's cell. What about *backlighting* it? Backlight would eliminate the problem of the transparency of the web in frontal light. With a dark background the strands should become silver and distinct, like frost on a window.

Fill-light from the front would be enough to give the spider definition. He made a note to call Wagner.

He moved on to an earlier note concerning the number of suitable bedrooms required for the vampire's attacks. Who was ever attacked by a vampire in the kitchen? The gowned figure, virginal and exposed, aslant on her bed or dreaming unaware at the window. . . . Voyeurism was the central thrill of the vampire-story. The heroine left to herself at night, with the vampire at the window, tapping to come in.

Vampirism was something private and hooded, beyond the individual's will to control. The arch—the cave-vault, the all-too-visible hiding place—should then be the visual leitmotif of the film. He made a few sketches.

When he finished, only thirty-five minutes had passed and he was no closer to going back to sleep. He sat gathering wool for some minutes. Then he dug out of his desk Galeen's treatment, which he hadn't yet had time to break down systematically.

## NoSferAtu: A TaLe of HoRroR
### by Henrik Galeen

The old peddler pulls his junk cart from house to house. He comes to a stop before a prim front door. Fortunate people must live here! A young couple opens the door.—"No thank you, we don't need anything!"—But the peddler refuses to leave. Oh: the beautiful young lady shows interest in the trinkets! Quickly he holds up a ring: a jackal's skull. Angrily the lady refuses. Again the trembling hand reaches into the boxes. An amulet: a bloated spider clutching a moth. The door begins to swing shut. No wonder, if he begins with death and spiders to a young couple in love! But now, now he has something else for the lovely lady. He holds up a brooch. The woman's eyes glow. Her husband cannot refuse her request; he buys it. Both gaze upon a tiny portrait in crimson enamel: a pelican suckling her young with her heart's blood.

The peddler says, "The symbol of love, and here—" he rummages in the lowest depths of his boxes "—a little book, as a bonus." He is already gone! The two, frightened, hold the book, on the cover of which are two entwined hearts, resplendent. A book for lovers? "Come, let me see." Timidly they open it. *A Chronicle of the Death Which Descended Upon Our City in Anno Domini 1839, and Its True Cause.*

The woman is furious and wants to throw the book away, but as if by the power of magic, a power which seems to radiate from the printed text, the eyes of both are fastened to it.

In the little town of the narrow streets and crooked gables live Thomas and Ellen Hutter, a happy young couple. Everything is bright and sunny around them. But there is Knock, Hutter's employer. And one day Knock produces a letter and speaks with disturbing intensity about a Count Orlok, who lives far away in Transylvania. Orlok wishes an address in their town, something "lovely and run-down." Through the window Knock indicates the sinister ruins across from the Hutter apartment: "Offer him this!"

Wanderlust! Hutter hurries home to take his leave of Ellen. He entrusts her to his friend Harding and departs. . . .

He spends the night in a Carpathian inn before he calls at the castle of the Count. An old book falls into his hands. In it he reads of Nosferatu, the vampire, born out of the blood of the sins of mankind. He wants to turn back, but is no longer able to. And so he enters the castle the following evening. Misgivings swarm about him. Slowly the gates open. In the dark entranceway a figure stands motionless. Waiting. A tremor grips the visitor, but there is no going back. Behind him the gates close.

In the morning he awakes in an easy chair. A wide hall extends around him. His senses swim. Where was he last night? Was not the master of this castle sitting across from him, in the other straight-backed chair? Were not marvelous foods steaming before him? Did not the master of the castle suck blood out of his hand and neck?

The next night. He flees through the castle like one persecuted. Quickly into his room. No bolt on the door. He hides himself in bed. A looming up of the world of horror, of frenzied murder and death, coming toward him, seizing him by the throat. A struggle. But as if the horror hears the terrified Ellen's faraway cry for her husband, it returns, slowly, to its sepulchral night.

But it is not exorcised. Its power grows. In the pre-dawn gloom Hutter sees an uncanny carriage in the castle courtyard, a black spectre carrying long, misshapen boxes, rough coffin upon rough coffin. Now he realizes: Ellen is in danger! And with the last of his strength he enacts his escape, down a sheer precipice.

From the east it draws near. In Galicia, in Varna, in Constantinople, wherever the mysterious ship moors, rats appear, and Death rages. The corpses have marks on their necks which no one can explain. The Plague is coming. It is a race between Hutter and his destiny. He hurries from town to town, lashed by fear, as if he could outrun the horror. Only one person is composed: Ellen. Knock has been committed to a madhouse.

The Death breaks out among the ship's crew. One after the other is wrapped in cloth and dropped into the sea. The captain and mate are finally alone. Then it gushes forth—black, like a terrible upwelling—rats and more rats. And behind them, the Nosferatu. Insanity in his face, the mate jumps overboard. The captain lashes himself to the wheel, and standing thus awaits the unthinkable.

The storm howls through the narrow streets of the little town. The sea stalks the shore like an enraged beast. A shadow overhangs the waves: a sail, a ship coming ever closer.

The storm abates. Noiselessly the ship glides into the harbor. It is still. Rats clamber from its hold. A form with a coffin walks forth.

In the madhouse Knock pulls himself up to the bars of his window, and murmurs: "The Master is near! The Master is near! . . ."

Hutter arrives that very night. Ellen! Ellen! Finally he presses her to his breast. But then he looks into her eyes: the joy has died away. He doesn't understand. Has the race not been won? Around her the glow of the room, but Ellen shakes her head, knowing that outside stands a form with poisonous rat's teeth which has been watching their window for a long time.

On the ship, no living creatures. At the wheel, the dead captain, his throat torn. The logbook. Plague! The drummer goes through the streets and spreads the news. Windows are closed. But the horror is not vanquished. It rages in the city. A man without hope chalks crosses on doors, the sign: no one lives here any longer.

Knock escapes from the madhouse. The anger of the masses turns on him.

In the book that Hutter has brought back from Transylvania, it is written: "Only when an innocent woman makes him forget the first crow of the cock will he disintegrate in the light." Ellen knows: it is not the Plague. In the ruin across the street it crouches, and every night its eyes stare across at her. . . .

In the night she comes to a decision. Sends her husband away. Opens the window. Watches it approach. It seizes her. Hands claw her body. Hour upon hour passes: the unholy bliss of devils. Suddenly, outside, the first crow of the cock. The ghastly hands try to free themselves. But she entwines herself more tightly around her tormentor. And there: the sun!

The horror rises up. Its limbs writhe and dissolve. It disintegrates in the light.

In its place, a pestilential mist, which itself disperses.

In the little room, the sun breaks through. "The knowing person has conquered the incomprehensible, at terrible cost."

Once again, the cozy corner in the little apartment belonging to the young pair. They have been sitting the entire night bent over the book, shaken by the tragedy

unrolling there before them. The morning is already dawning!

Both stare with unseeing eyes, dread in their expressions.
But the husband gathers his courage and hurries to the window. Opens it! The young day gilds the crooked gables of
the town!

"Come, my love, let us enjoy the light—!" With a single
motion he takes the book and brooch and flings both
emphatically out the window. They embrace.

Life has claimed them again!

He spent a few minutes dealing with his despair at the amount
of work still to be done. A few moments seemed inspired. Others
seemed wrongheaded. Films born in the head expired on paper,
only to be revived in the shooting and editing, like those Oriental
paper flowers that bloom when placed in water.

It was five-thirty. Below, in the kitchen, the teapot whistled
faintly.

He had breakfast with *The History of Witchcraft*. Frau Reger
served, with an occasional glance at the illustrations. Her expression was that of a nanny who'd found her charge sitting in his own
waste. Spiess remained asleep.

Murnau was getting ready to leave when Spiess finally stirred.
He usually made large, groaning sounds. It brought to mind animals at a water hole.

Murnau had an appointment with Lasker-Schüler. One of the
film's backers had been balking at the lack of receipts and
accounting. Why there *was* a lack of receipts and accounting
wasn't clear; on that point Grau was evasive. The backer was an
entrepreneur of ladies' shoes named Agnuzzo, who had recently
let slip that he had for years been smitten with Else Lasker-
Schüler. Grau had immediately used Murnau to arrange a meeting. A bad idea, since she detested that sort of thing.

During the drive into town, Murnau brooded about Hans. The chauffeur was a beautiful and silent boy named Huber. The car was an American Ford, maroon and cream.

He and Lasker-Schüler had been largely out of touch for over a year, for one reason or another. She always needed money. Her novel was still selling and her verse play had had a healthy run, but she was endlessly cheated, and spent money the way she did everything else, refusing to calculate the consequences.

She and Paul lived in pensions and, occasionally, cafés. Often she was evicted from her table for failing to place an order. He'd heard she'd been caught with her hand on a financier's billfold, and had escaped by claiming it had been guided by an archangel. She'd been arrested at the Zoo Station for being a public nuisance, orating for coins in what she claimed was Arabian.

They had agreed to meet at the Romanische. On the opposite side of the square, the Kaiser Wilhelm Church was ringed with street peddlers. Traffic was bumptious and squawky. On the sidewalk, table artists dashed off caricatures in which everyone ended up looking like Conrad Veidt. Most of the customers were schoolboy bohemians, with the occasional young girl with her Modern Woman haircut and copy of *Die Koralle* thrown in.

Lasker-Schüler was inside, in a telephone booth yelling into the receiver. He assumed he knew what she was up to. The week before, one of the Mosse papers had published a *Where Are They Now?* piece claiming that her destitution had reduced her to having Paul sell picture postcards from table to table. This looked like her way of negotiating a retraction with the features editor.

She hammered the receiver against the mahogany booth and then shouted back into it. They didn't know what they'd done to her! Now shithead tourists from the Ku'damm came round just to offer food. She was like a nature park.

She calmed to listen to their explanation. She should kill them, she finally said. She should come to their bed at night and lay them open from chin to breastbone. She'd find their address. Did they hear her?

A young English couple viewed the performance with delight. This was why they'd come to Berlin. Lasker-Schüler offered them a cupped breast.

She slammed the phone down and stepped from the booth. She smiled. On the way over to him, she flopped down at a table from which three boys from military school had been staring. She moved her hand before one as if conjuring something out of his face. "O fortunate child," she chanted. "I am an Oriental Daughter of Joy."

When she stood they hooted for her to stay. Murnau met her halfway to his table and she gave him a hug. She was damp with sweat and a foot shorter. "If it isn't Ulrich the Helmet," she said.

For a while Hans had started in on her nickname game, as well. He'd called Murnau Bayard, the Knight Without Reproach.

She looked lovely, Murnau told her.

And didn't Paul? she wanted to know. Paul sat miserably in the far corner, drawing.

She loved him completely, she lamented, and yet she dragged him into these filthy holes.

He was using a blue pencil on an oversized art pad. Hans had been so impressed with his talent and moved by his plight that he'd left a thousand marks in his will to further the boy's training. The money had long since disappeared, only God knew where.

She still had beautiful skin. She was wearing a leather cap, and the heat made her face shimmer with perspiration. Bracelets of turquoise and tourmaline jangled from her elbows to her wrists.

What air the Romanische provided, submarine crews would have found insupportable. She pulled up a chair. Murnau pulled over another, for Agnuzzo. "Who's that for?" she asked. "Hans?"

"I'm sorry," she said when he didn't respond.

Paul came over and joined them. She asked how Murnau had been sleeping. She'd written about him that his insomnia made him as dull as a block of wood and as restless as a forest animal. She had something for him, she said, and pulled from a rucksack beneath the table a leaflet advertising a lecture by a Dr. Knax on "Wanking as Mass Murder." She was always teasing him like that.

When he asked what news she had, she told him that the day before she'd experienced a transformation into a Negress from primordial times. On her body had been printed a message in an unknown alphabet.

"The people behind us in line were alarmed," Paul added.

She wanted to know what it was like working with Grau. She didn't much like him, and called him the Gateway to the Occult. Still, she was curious because he was intense and secretive and provincial. His paintings had a disturbing and sinister dissociative pith to them, like Kubin's.

Grau had been the one who approached Murnau with the idea of Nosferatu. Murnau had invited him to go ahead with the attempt to raise money. The idea of that creature of the shadows—twenty-one or -two, beetle-legged, long-faced, with the hands of an arboreal animal—as a successful film producer astounded him.

On his pad, Paul drew a long, narrow face with fangs.

Murnau said he didn't know where to begin. He told her that Grau was forever having to restrain himself from hugging someone. He had visionary ecstasies of the sort associated with high fever.

This was the sort of thing Lasker-Schüler always heard about herself.

Was he genuinely connected to the spirit world? she asked.

He owned his own copy of the Malleus Maleficarum, Murnau told her.

She was delighted with the prospect of the utterly rational Murnau having to wrestle with a spook-chaser.

They were quiet during the saucer-rattling noise of the elevated S-Bahn. Murnau looked around for Agnuzzo.

"And what about you?" he asked. "How have you been doing?"

She outlined her latest legal wrangle, involving an attempt to secure a small inheritance from her father. Her father had been a prosperous banker from Elberfeld. She traditionally spoke of her youth as a lost paradise of peace and security, yet was fond of relating that as a four-year-old she'd climbed onto her roof from a third-floor window and called out to passersby below, "I'm so bored!"

While she talked, he exchanged a smile with her son. Paul was happy here, left alone to draw and think, away from the boys with their leather balls and fistfights.

You're thinking of your own life now, he reminded himself.

"Speaking of Spiess," Lasker-Schüler remarked apropos of nothing.

"You know he's moved in?" Murnau finally replied. Everything about where this was headed seemed tiresome and unproductive.

He gave her the short version. He'd been alone since Mary Degele had died. The house was too big for one.

"It was sad about Mary," she said.

He agreed. In the last years, he told her, there'd been a heartbreaking aspect of guilt to her despair, as if something she'd left undone had caused Hans's death.

Lasker-Schüler was silent.

They both looked at Paul, having forgotten how much the subject still hurt him.

Spiess was painting the study and both bedrooms, Murnau explained. As part of his agreement for living there.

How was it for him, being there? she asked.

His old apartment had been uninhabitable, Murnau told her. Piles of drawing pads, laundry, soup pots and grills, loose tools, enigmatic and unmatched bicycle parts. His canvases, finished and unfinished. His easel toward the end had straddled the sink.

"And how is it for you?" she asked quietly. Meaning: how was it having him in Hans's house?

"Have you noticed," she asked, "how many of your films have involved a couple jeopardized by a third figure who's sinister, ambiguous, and male?"

"I didn't know you practiced film criticism now," Murnau said.

"Don't fight," Paul said. They looked at him and apologized. Lasker-Schüler sighed.

Spiess's nostrils had always been wet, she remembered. Whenever she ran into him, she was always telling him to wipe his nose.

They let it rest with that image. Whenever they seemed about to make eye contact, one of them looked away. Paul excused himself to go to the bathroom. Murnau by this point assumed that Agnuzzo wasn't coming.

She asked about Slovakia. It was strewn with fortresses, he told her. It was the perfect place to locate exteriors for the Undead. The Carpathians were too far away. In one town there was an absolute Doré illustration of a ruin, and nearby were mountain ranges out of Friedrich's early work. They were using as their guiding image for the project a portrait they'd found, all pallor and spidery hands, of a Celsissimus Princeps Esterházy. Justice was represented over his head by scales and a huge scimitar. The local inns were cheap. The cemeteries in the mountain villages had no walls and spread into fields or bordered the roadside.

"Do you remember," Lasker-Schüler asked, "the fondness he had for that Arabic dish, with the eggs?"

"Hans," Murnau said. She nodded. He'd loved eggs cooked all night in onion peel. It imparted to them the gentle flavor and color of the onion.

She said she'd known about them from the first moment she'd seen them together. Did he remember? Mary had introduced them in the back garden—here was her boy's Frisian friend, the one everyone was always trying to get to smile.

An Adonis, Murnau said. Tall and slim, with northern features and beautiful red-blond hair.

A skinny overgrown boy, Lasker-Schüler said. Trying to bury his infinite inhibitions behind a mask of who knew what.

"Have you been working on my epitaph?" he asked.

"On everyone's, in fact," she said.

"Jussuf, Prince of Thebes!" one of the schoolboys called over. The other boys swooned away from him. "Come to my tent! My heart fetches roses from your mouth."

She took no notice of being quoted. She said she'd told Hans, when he'd asked what she thought of his new friend, *There's* a boy uninterruptedly at work upon himself.

"What did he say to that?" Murnau asked.

She shrugged.

"When did he ever judge anyone harshly?" she asked.

They looked off together toward the bathroom. "That's why Paul loved him so much," he said. "When someone said something cutting, he was always so helpless. He couldn't speak that language."

He experienced an unrelated visual memory: instead of replacing broken laces, Hans retied them. The fronts of his shoes looked like festivals of bows.

He smiled as if the trace of someone were the same thing as his presence.

Hans had had to absorb his hypochondria, his sulks, his domestic crises. They once went round to shops for half a day to replace some missing Brazilian coffee.

Hans had called Murnau's sore throats symptoms of the basic untruthfulness of his life.

The three military boys stopped by on their way out. They expressed their sorrow that Lasker-Schüler hadn't risen to their offer. They would've shown her a good time.

She thanked them and asked them to please go away.

The two of them waited for Paul. Talking about Hans made her visibly more impatient with Murnau. He knew she blamed him for Hans's presence in the Army in the first place. She'd tried to talk him out of joining up when she'd first heard what Murnau had done. After Hans had been killed, she'd responded to one of Murnau's distraught letters with, *So now it's Murnau the Ascetic, cut off from the world. Even his best friends cannot understand his grief. Well. Get over it. Everyone goes home to his dead heart.*

She seemed to be reading his face. "I always meant to ask you," she said. "Did you know what his last letters to me were like? Did he ever write to you about suicide?"

He looked at her. He was without speech. The door had swung open onto a plain.

"I thought you'd known," she said. "I thought you'd known about it."

Something blocked the light. Someone was standing over them, sweating.

Agnuzzo. When Paul came back to the table, the two of them stood looking at one another.

Agnuzzo asked for forgiveness. First one cab, then another had broken down. Who were the mechanics who maintained such wrecks? He'd nearly run the last hundred meters.

He turned to Lasker-Schüler, extending a hand, and said he was honored.

She pointed at him, looking at Murnau. "Who is this?" she asked.

Murnau had his hands on each side of his head to hold it where it was. The café righted itself. "This is Herr Agnuzzo," he said with some hoarseness.

Agnuzzo explained that he had the privilege of having invested in Herr Murnau's most recent film.

Lasker-Schüler stood, her eyes lowered as if in shyness. Paul looked at her, waiting. *"And my lips parted in shy hesitation,"* she

recited. *"Like poisonous flowers that do the devil's bidding . . ."*
She ran her palms up Agnuzzo's shirtfront, took a collar in each
fist, and pulled. Buttons pinged around the room. Agnuzzo's shirt
was opened to the sternum. "Sodomite!" she called. "Creature of
Darkness!" She let him go, then retrieved her rucksack, crossed
her arms against his taint, and left the table with Paul.

Agnuzzo recovered his poise and looked at Murnau with
delight. Murnau looked back, his hands still propping up his head.
All aspects of Agnuzzo's expression made clear that the meeting
had been everything that he'd been hoping for and more.

# NOSFERATU, EINE SYMPHONIE DES GRAUENS

# EXTERIORS

Six weeks of exteriors: the Carpathians, the Baltic towns of Wismar, Rostock, and Lübeck, as well as ocean vistas of Heligoland and the Frisian Islands in the North Sea. All shooting, exterior and interior, must be finished by November 1921. We begin here, in Czechoslovakia. Half the company has yet to arrive; those who have are filled with questions. Nothing of course has gone as planned. To add to the confusion there are my daily visits to foreign doctors, to say nothing of the visits of nurses to me. What time I have is often expended in elegiac dreams about H———. But already the film takes me from the soft anguish of idleness and drives me from any room where I cannot work.

7/12/21. This is intended to be for the patient readers of *Der Querschnitt* the journal of a filmmaker's progress: an ongoing chronicle, from rough notes composed day to day, of the trials and tribulations of this new project. I hereby pledge to do my utmost to prevent this diary from becoming a "melancholy school of posturing and dreary self-deception." Frankness and clarity will be the goals. If I will not, cannot be truthful with myself here, where can I be?

With this film, I will not aim at poetry. I will try to build a table. It will be for you to eat at it, criticize it, chop it up for firewood.

It seems appropriate in this confessional form to chronicle the beginnings of my slide from the status of a young man of promise into the regrettable position of filmmaker. Early in 1914, with my career in the theater—specifically, with Max Reinhardt's prestigious troupe—all but assured, I drifted into a moving-picture show to see the American D. W. Griffith's *Judith of Bethulia*. I was mesmerized by the giant figure of the wine-guzzling Holofernes, who towered over everyone. Where had they found him? In some circus, I supposed. I mentioned this to Reinhardt, who laughed and told me that the same actor had visited Germany a year earlier, and was shorter than he was. He had been made to *seem* huge by Griffith's camera. Reinhardt had had no idea how. He suggested I write to Billy Bitzer, Griffith's cameraman. I was possessed by the trick, and would have, had the war not intervened. I was twenty-five and as curious as a field dog about everything having to do with filmmaking.

In the 1914 war, I served in the Air Corps, and came to understand aviation as a new way of seeing. (The air arm itself grew out of the reconnaissance service.) Airborne vision now escaped that Euclidian tyranny so acutely felt by the ground troops in the trenches; in this new, astounding topological field, air pilots already had their own special-effects, with their own names: loops, figure-eights, falling-leaf rolls. My understanding was transformed by the way the airborne observer's hand seemed to detach itself from the body and stretch out in freedom . . . the aerial body, looking down from a great height. . . . Good training for the fledgling film director.

After the war I bought a battered old view camera and tripod in a Charlottenburg junk shop and began shooting pictures of everything within range. I even attempted to develop and print the footage myself in a converted coat closet. The experiment was not a success.

Eventually I progressed in the only way possible for me, which was to make every mistake until there were no mistakes left to make, and the right way of proceeding was the only possibility remaining. Like many of the early filmmakers, I thought myself an urbane bohemian and outsider, eager to experiment, one of the sensitive, nervous spirits of the age, a tinkerer and a visionary with what I hoped was a keen business sense.

Even then the film world, to my dismay, did not fall prostrate before me. The truth was that I would have to become a bit less gangly and awkward, at least enough to overcome the distressing habit of falling over my feet, before I could impress that world with the idea that I was a gifted artist drawing on vast resources of experience and sophistication.

DOLNY´ KUBI´N, Slovakia. Grau wants the names of Stoker's characters changed, but echoed. Harker has thus become Hutter. On the long trip here I wrote the first title from his diary, which will introduce the story: *Nosferatu. Doesn't the name sound like the midnight call of a death bird? Beware of uttering it, or the pictures of life will turn to pale shadows, nightmares will rise up from the heart and nourish themselves on your blood.* [Fade in a long shot of the town.] *For a long time I have been meditating on the rise and fall of the Great Death in my father's town of Wisborg. Here is the story of it: In Wisborg there lived a man named Hutter with his young wife, Ellen.*

WANGENHEIM WAS a compromise choice as Hutter. I wanted Veidt, whom Grau proclaimed too old, too sinister-looking, and, he might have added, too intimately associated with me. Neither of us is happy with Wangenheim, but he was available. At the first production meeting, he looks over the room assignments and complains that the rooms have been apportioned hierarchically. The top floor, the one with the view, has been divided between art director Albin Grau, cameraman Fritz Arno Wagner, scenarist Henrik Galeen, and myself. Everyone looks to me to quash this kind of petty revolt. Wangenheim offers his chin and makes a

face. He's a left-winger and an aristocrat and probably feels isolated in this crew.

There *is* a hierarchy, I inform him. I congratulate him for having noticed. The arrangement is so our collaboration can continue at any and all hours. Grau, handing out room keys, suggests
he spend less time worrying about accommodations and more
worrying about his performance. Wangenheim then wants to
know why his room is below Spiess's, and why in fact Spiess has
been brought along. One of those film company spats, unpleasantness tinged with subtextual insinuation. Why was there
scrimping and saving on one end and splurging on the other?
Spiess, I remind everyone, has lived in the east and could prove
invaluable. The usual grumbling before the rebel angels retreat,
quiescent for now and more trouble later.

THE COMPANY, like a class of children, never understands: it's
not a matter of severity or love, but devotion to the work at hand.
Behind my back, they poke fun at my unwillingness to show emotion even in disagreements. It is simple, simple, simple: by remaining master of myself, I remain master of the company. This is all I
need to remember. Without that first mastery, all other authority
is quickly at an end.

PERSISTENT THOUGHTS of H——. Lasker-Schüler claims to
have no more information. Have I tried everyone else? Are there
memory-tricks that would release new answers?

(—RECORD EVERYTHING; revise later with Q in mind.)

. . .

THE WEEK before we left, *Der Film* finally announced the founding of the Prana Film company, with a remaining capital of twenty thousand marks, the rest already having been spent. Two managers were named: Enrico Dieckmann, a merchant in Berlin-Lichterfelde, and Albin Grau, an artist/painter in Berlin. The name of the company was explained (the reference was to the Buddhist concept *prana*, "vital breath") and attributed to Grau, who, we were informed, "reflects a great deal on the occult aspects of life." Accompanying the announcement was a list of nine films (!) scheduled for production next year, each illustrated with a drawing of Grau's. At the very bottom in small print we learned that directing Prana's first production, *Nosferatu, a Symphony of Horrors*, would be one F. W. Murnau. "Artistic direction"—apparently a separate category—would be handled by Albin Grau. "Together," the announcement concluded with a wan and affecting flourish, "they propose to construct the film on new principles."


WE'RE FILMING in Dolny´ Kubín for the scenes involving the inn in the Carpathians. A dismal, crooked little town perched like a tooth on a hill. Father would say, "What kind of work would take you to a place like this?" I imagine him, when people ask, answering only: "He's in Slovakia." H—— would be pleased to hear me imagining Father's thoughts, after all this estrangement.

The castle, Oravsky Zamok, is not far from town. Wagner discovered it months ago, and sent a postcard. It was built on the river Orava in the thirteenth century, high on a curiously hollowed-out rock. The most elevated part is a watchtower that overhangs the Orava by more than one hundred meters. The watchtower, shot against the light, will form the final image of the shadow of the vampire passing from the earth.

Tomorrow we begin shooting on the dilapidated terrace, with

Wangenheim, who so far has had only useless ideas as to his portrayal of Hutter.

Still awake. This preparation, most of my life since December: how much does it avail me now?

We start with Hutter discovering the marks on his neck, writing Ellen. It will be in bright sunlight, against a ruined stone wall. We must make certain the vines have been cleared from the battlement. We must counter excess shadow with lamps. We must be ready should the weather not cooperate. If the terrace scene comes off we'll go on to Hutter's search for the coffin. After the arch I'll pass in and do the stairway, to the right of where he sees the bolted door leading down . . .


SLEEPLESS, I wander the corridors. Napoleon said he made his battle plans from the fighting spirit of his sleeping soldiers.

Before the shooting, one must put oneself into a state of intense ignorance and curiosity, and yet see things *in advance*. My working method is to sketch out everything and then be completely open to impulse and improvisation. Recognize the true by its efficiency and power. The film's beauty will not be in the images (postcardism) but in the ineffable qualities that those images emanate. To use prodigious, heaven-sent machines merely for belaboring something fraudulent—how would that appear, in fifty years' time? And yet it's from those mechanisms that emotion will be born. Think of the great pianists. (Bach, answering an admiring pupil: "It's only a matter of striking the right notes at exactly the right moment.") We evoke the pre-industrial world of superstition by creating an illusion that allows the viewer to forget the film's technical base.

In the darkness and stillness there are murmurs and flickering light under Grau's door. I knock softly, and enter.

Grau and Galeen are sitting cross-legged around a guttering

candle. When they lean to make a point, shadows bend around the recesses of the room. Still uninvited, I sit. They share a bottle of Hungarian wine. We can hear mice gnawing at the walls' interior. Grau repeats his story of the old peasant with whom he was billeted in the Army. The peasant was convinced that his father, who died without receiving the sacraments, haunted the village in the form of a vampire. He showed Grau an official document about a man named Morowitch, exhumed in Progatza in 1884. The body showed no signs of decomposition, and the teeth were strangely long and sharp, and protruded from the mouth. The man was proclaimed undead, known in Serbia as the Nosferatu. Grau an ardent spiritualist. His next project, he's informed us, will be something called *Höllenträume: Dreams of Hell.*

Galeen, too, has a vampire story, from a cousin who served in Austria-Hungary. Galeen is slightly off-putting, watchful and disquieting. He has a bulbous face, with lank brown hair, skin like an orange rind, and an odd and pointless smile. He is only twenty-nine, four years younger than Grau and myself, and was born in Berlin. He reacted well to my revision of his treatment. He's a Rosicrucian; perhaps even one of the adepts. I learned that from others.

He tells us the following, in his smooth voice: After it had been reported in a nearby village that a vampire had killed three men by sucking their blood, Galeen's cousin was, by high decree of the local Honorable Supreme Command, sent there to investigate, along with two subordinate medical officers. This is the story they were told: Only days after the funeral of a girl by the name of Stana, eighteen years old, who had died in childbirth two weeks previous, and who had announced in a fever that she had painted herself with the blood of a vampire, the family caught sight of the deceased sitting on the front steps of her house. The dead girl repeatedly appeared afterwards at night in the street, and knocked on doors. Children sickened and died. She had relations with an addled widower. When at night, like a trail of fog, she would leave a farm, she left a dead man in her wake.

Galeen's cousin and the other officers were taken to the grave-yard to open and examine the grave. When they exhumed her, she was whole and intact with blood flowing from her nose, mouth, and ears. When the girl's mother saw her, she spat and said, "You are to disappear; don't get up again and don't move!" At those words tears flowed from the corpse's eyes. After seeing that, the villagers pulled her from the grave, cut her into pieces, and tied them with cloth. The cloth they threw on a thornbush which they set on fire. Whereupon a strong wind rose and blew after them, howling, all the way back to the village.

THE FIRST day is overcast. It's always a question of the intensity of the light. Wagner's assistants test it with orange filter glasses. We wait. At eleven I announce we'll set up the close-ups. For those we don't need sunlight. No sooner are we ready than the sun is out. We go on, but now Wangenheim and Greta are squinting; Wagner and his assistants have to screen with canvas the very sun we've been waiting for all day, fake the half-light we've suffered through to this point. Flies circle everywhere. The wind shakes a background I want still. The camera develops a tremor. Wangenheim abominable.

THAT NIGHT, cold sweats while trying to sort out the next day's tasks. Confronted by the characters, I feel like an official called in to oversee a crowd of immigrants. They stand about, passive, as I regard them with growing dismay.

DAY 2: more camera troubles. Drove off at nine in the morning. Spectacular trip. Stopped at a wine tavern, then continued off the main road to show Spiess the avenue of Caspar David Friedrich trees Grau showed me earlier. Pointed out to him as well the pitched waterfall Hutter will see from his room in the castle the night of the greatest danger. Every time I view the place it's a revelation. Spiess astounded. The grottoes and clefts and riot of overhanging branches enclosed us within the sound and force of the cataract. We could see movement flitting above in the narrow and overgrown cliff faces. We were in a world where all was wonder, delicate and secret, and beside which all our clutter looked like a farce in bad taste. On the way home by a different route, I was talking to Spiess about the second inn, where Hutter is warned against proceeding to the castle, and round a bend all in one glance I recognized, down to the smallest detail, the exact setting I had resigned myself to having to build. Here were the windows for Hutter's view of the frightened horses, the old shutters with the carved hex signs, the doors and boxed-in bed, the stone well, the apples piled in an oaken bucket, everything! The interiors as good as the exteriors, with this quality of the luminous strangeness of the ordinary shining through the walls. . . .

SPIESS, TOO, is fascinated with the lore of vampires. He reads a number of Slavic languages, and has helped with the forbidding and disintegrating texts Galeen has pulled from the local libraries. We never have enough background material, and what we find always feels too vague. At night, sitting on my bed in my room, Spiess reports, his voice transforming the softest consonants into sounds that make my neck ache with desire. Among the Slavs it's reported that one may strew ashes or salt around headstones in a cemetery to determine, by looking for footprints later, if any of the bodies are leaving their graves at night. If a grave is sunk in, or if a cross has taken a crooked position, the deceased has transformed himself. Often there is visible a hole in the grave from which the vampire emerges. And the Gypsies believe that if dogs are barking, no vampires are in the village, but if dogs are silent, then the vampires have come.

WITH THIS sort of story, everything, Wegener wrote when he was working on his *Golem*, depends on a certain flow in which the fantastic world of the past rejoins the world of the present. And yet how does one make judgments about emotional truth in such situations? Authenticity is a problem that remains unresolved in this country. Transylvania, with its evocative meaning ("beyond the forest") seems appropriate as our setting: that place which can only be imagined. Europe's unconscious.

REMEMBER TO flag sections to be excised for *Querschnitt*.

ONE OF Wagner's assistants is spending the week filming the light at dawn (real) on the castle gates (constructed). His task is to open on a fade every morning until "morning's dawn" becomes "morning horror": *Morgengrau* becomes *Morgengrauen*. I have a specific effect in mind, and this stock can capture it. Then he'll be sent home to film the dilapidated salt storehouses of Lübeck, for the long shots of the Bremen house of the vampire. All those empty window-sockets, with their uncanny anthropomorphic quality.

DINNERS WITH Spiess and Wagner help us clarify our ideas. The shot is not a painting, dependent only upon the expressive content of its static composition; it's also a space negotiable in every way, open to intrusion and transformation, inviting the most unpredictable courses. It's necessary to understand the process by which the mood and tone of such spaces can change. If only the camera could move! If the question becomes not only "what is the image?" but also "how does it change?" we exploit precisely that connection between film and dream; spaces shift with the logic and fluidity of the dream state. The geography of the film must be evocative yet elusive; the vampire's castle and the wilderness concrete in their tone and unmappable in their contours. Reality, but with fantasy; they must dovetail.

Spiess agreed. Wagner offered in support the reminder that in Rubens's engraving of the sheep, which Goethe showed to Eckermann, the shadow is on the same side as the sun.

IF ONLY the camera could move! Imagine if the camera could move! Wagner is every bit as excited about the possibilities. "When and if," he says dryly, "we have the budget to experiment accordingly."

SECOND FULL production meeting tonight. All of us—Wagner, Grau, Spiess, Galeen, myself, Max Schreck, who will be playing the Nosferatu—crowded into my room. Some wine and sausage. Talking about the sources of horror. Grau claims our new art has an advantage over literature because the image can be clear and concrete even as it remains inconceivable. This is the paradox that causes the hair on the back of our necks to rise. Wagner adds that what people look for in film is a way to load their imagination with strong images. The fact that these images are silent is a supplementary attraction; they're silent like dreams. I think he's right, for as Hofmannsthal points out, only apparently have we forgotten our dreams; in fact there's not a single dream that, reawakened, does not begin to stir: the dark corner, the breath of air, the face of an animal, the glide of an unfamiliar gait, all of it makes the presence of dreams perceptible. The blackness below the stairs to the cellar, the barrel filled with rainwater in the courtyard, the door to the granary, the door to the loft, the neighbor's door through which the beautiful woman casts into the dark and palpitating depths of the child's heart an unexpected thrill of desire . . .

We fall silent, passing the wine. Spiess says it's like traveling through the air in the company of Asmodeus, the demon who raised roofs and laid bare all secrets.

Wagner says he imagines a future film which will be nothing on screen but beautiful creatures and transparent gestures, looks in which the entire soul is read.

Grau points out that in Mediterranean countries, children born with red hair or unusually pale complexions were watched carefully for other vampiric signs. Everyone looks at me.

Galeen has been listening to all of this, his elbow on the arm of his chair, his palm cupping his fat face. It's necessary, he says, to correct the dictionaries. The majority of terms today no longer correspond to the ideas whose image they were intended to provide. Are love, friendship, heart, and soul still the same concepts as when the ancient dictionaries were composed? What do the old "fantastic" worlds of Grimm, Hoffmann, or Poe represent for us today? Let us, he says, consider them with modern eyes: they remain a source of inspiration, nothing more; for what we have daily before us goes beyond even Jules Verne. Douglas Fairbanks's flying carpet already bores today's young; they sniff out special-effects and look for the artifice that made it possible. We're no longer astonished by the technically unheard-of. We're surprised on those days the newspaper does not trumpet new break-throughs. So we look for the fantastic within ourselves. We notice the child or the dog who walks to the mirror, caught by the miracle of this doubled face. We wonder: If this second self, the Other, were to come out of the mirror's frame? . . . .

Empty wine bottles are pyramided on their sides against the wall like artillery rounds. Grau, slightly drunk, eyes Spiess. There's been further tension due to his presence on the payroll. Prana, as a new production company, can afford little extravagance, according to Grau. This despite the fact that Agnuzzo's delight with Lasker-Schüler caused him to pony up a check to cover "additional contingencies."

In Berlin, Grau quarreled to the last minute about the additional spending represented by Spiess. He stalked around the station platform gesturing with the company's train tickets in his hands, and gave in only when I reminded him how much money I'd already saved by agreeing to cast Wangenheim instead of Veidt. Grau is ambitious, and given to wild statements intended to cow the listener. Prana is a creation of his will and rhetoric and is all he has. His painting career has not been a success. I told him Spiess was indispensable to my thinking, and my dreaming, and important to the project in ways I could not yet articulate. Grau finally accepted my explanation. Spiess remains uncomfortable in his presence.

Wagner peers into an empty bottle. Grau is slumped to the floor, his head against the door of a low cupboard. Galeen still has his chin in his hands. Only Schreck seems unaffected by the wine, looking each of us over in turn.

The meeting has petered out. To finish, we toast the enterprise: Grau the good fortune of the company, Galeen the spirits around us who work with us, Schreck the Undead, Wagner the new cameras ordered from Berlin, and myself my young collaborator Spiess and his contribution to my work. In the silence, Spiess's eyes shy from mine. Afterwards, he's the last to leave. He stands with his back to me, rummaging in the mess for his coat. He's still angry that I hadn't wanted him to come. I'm condemned not for having been unreasonable but for having come to my senses too slowly. I stand closer, still without touching him, and he eludes my hand nimbly, like a beautiful animal. I'm reminded of a title for which I can't find a place in the film: *She stands in front of him, still drawing back but trying to attract him to her.*

THIS HAS become something unsuitable for public consumption. Where will I get the $ to repay the advance?

SPIESS REFUSES to talk about Lasker-Schüler's claim. We quarrel about this regularly. He notes only that its savagery indicates how badly I must have hurt her. He offers no further insight on this point, either. So my detective work is solitary and intermittent. Hans is the roundtable topic of my insomnia. I work through our time together the way a limited art student toils to copy a masterpiece. And what does all that effort represent? A man, frustrated, weeping for himself.

I HAVE always been a fugitive and a vagabond. For a thousand years none of our family has remained anywhere without growing uneasy, without being seized by wanderlust. I am at home in no house and in no country.

The Plumpes have always been aloof, have always designed their own worlds. My father left a thriving business and went his own way, bought a magnificent estate at Wilhelmshöhe, with land, hunting, a carriage, and a horse. We children were delighted. The garden had everything we could wish for—a grotto, a ruin, a secret pond, a giant stone, a trapeze. It was a miniature paradise.

Bernhard was the first to visit me in Berlin after I'd cut off communication. The first night I joked with him about Father letting his youngest son out in Sodom, and he told me he'd been strictly forbidden to move in my "circles." When we met Spiess by accident, Bernhard took his leave, and did not meet me as planned the next morning.

I am both my father and Something Else, and remain mute before the ongoing miracle of the coexistence of the two.

TALKED WITH Schreck about the Nosferatu. Schreck is a very strange man: narrow-shouldered, peculiarly stiff and clumsy, strikingly ugly without any makeup. At lunch he knocked over his water glass with a wooden sweep of his arm and then simply watched it, glared at me and then the water as it ran across the table. Intensely private, yet he's begun to follow me around, trying to absorb as much as he can. His performance is absolutely crucial. He has had very little experience, but when I saw him bending without pleasure over a child on the Kurfürstendamm I knew he was the Nosferatu. I have begun talking with him about his role the only way I know how: trying to articulate the sources of my own obsessions. His silences seem equal parts hostility and understanding.

I talked of the vampire's parasitism—*you must die if I am to live.* I talked of the loathsomeness and the dread of his allure. I talked of how the terrible inhumanness of him, the nightmarish repulsiveness, should move easily among the bourgeois naturalism of the costumes and acting styles of the rest of the cast—how everyone must see him as in some ways *not out of the ordinary.*

MORE MIDNIGHT work with Spiess on Galeen's script while the rest of the company sleeps. The hotel is silent. In the distance someone is drawing a wagon up the road.

Spiess reports quietly on his readings. He lays out on the bed charcoal drawings of amulets and charms, diabolic designs. The vampire, he believes, first appears in a Serbian manuscript of the thirteenth century in which a *vuklodlak* is described as a creature which devours the sun and moon while chasing clouds. Among the contemporary Slavs, *vampir* and *vuklodlak* (literally, wolf's hair) are synonymous. He reads aloud from a fragment of fifteenth-century Turkish apocrypha: "The Force of Destruction is always near man and follows him like his shadow. For this reason man must always be restored. This restoration occurs in various forms: through the tears of the Force of Creation: water (bathing and washing); through the breath of the Force of Creation: air (ventilation of the house, and living outside); and through meeting every morning the first life-giving rays of the Force of Creation (which are sent from the sun)."

We trade ideas until the sky pales, building together an artifice superior to the work of either of our imaginations alone. We construct a new scene for Hutter's arrival: Distant mountains. Vratna Pass. In the background the fantastic castle of the Nosferatu in the evening light. A steep road leading straight up into the sky. Hutter abandoned by his coach. Something comes racing down—a carriage? A phantasm?—with unearthly speed and disappears behind a groundswell. Out of nowhere, reappears. Stops dead. Two black horses, their legs invisible, covered by black funeral cloth. Their eyes like pointed stars. Steam from their mouths. The coachman, whose face we cannot see. Hutter inside. Carriage drives at top speed through a *white* forest! (We'll use meters of negative, like "the land the sun travels through at night" so feared in ancient Egypt.)

If the camera could move *with* the coach, so we could feel the terrifying capacities of evil. . . .

Then the courtyard. The carriage at a halt. Almost in a faint, Hutter climbs down. As if in a whirlpool, the carriage circles round him and disappears. Then, very slowly, the two wings of the gate open up. . . .

.　.　.

SIX DAYS of shooting. The camera still trembles. The new one sent from Berlin is even worse. I let them develop the bad takes in case the camera has performed some miracle of its own. Yet some scenes come off beautifully. The panicking horses Hutter sees from the window of the inn. On a grassy slope, the ground falling away toward the back. Night mists creep up the valley. The horses raise their heads as if frightened and, scattering, gallop away. The white horse spun and shook perfectly, which he refused to do yesterday. The camera just got it. And one, after hours of work, *backed out* of the frame! The effect was marvelous. Even Wagner, for all his exhaustion, was excited by how it will look. The possibility of other people's fatigue never occurs to me.

SPIESS PROPOSES a trip to the South Seas to collaborate on an old photoplay of his entitled *The Island of the Demons*. I'm insufficiently excited about the idea. A horrible fight.

I MUST avoid a certain kind of coldness that results from the way I work. It would be fatal.

SPIESS GONE to Berlin for a few days for "personal matters." We fought again over Hans. Clumsy life going about its stupid work: even when we want to reveal ourselves we're so poor at it that we spend most of our time in self-concealment of one sort or another. My experience of him is discontinuous, my attention uneven, my judgment and understanding uncertain.

He was gone all night and announced his trip the next morning. I said nothing, and was busy the entire day. That afternoon on his pillow in his room, I left for him one of the vampire's entreaties to Hutter:

*Would you not like to wait awhile with me, dearest worthy? It is not so long until the sunrise—*

*And during the day I sleep my best; I sleep most truly, the deepest sleep—*

LONG HOURS in the makeshift projection room last night. The coach arriving at the inn. Wangenheim crossing the little bridge to the "land of the phantoms." The forest he views on his journey. That last setup particularly difficult because of the terrain. Extreme long shots of landscape must be shot north or south so that the crosslight provides definition. Flat, dead-on light causes shadows to fall away behind objects so that there's no modeling, and backlighting is problematic in all but the clearest skies.

It's irritating to see so little, because the true rhythms will be produced only in the cutting. Can't find the take of the white horse turning with its balked jumpiness, and there's no trace of it on the labels. Awful if that shot lost.

With some of the vistas Wagner hasn't enough courage. He compromises and won't take a bold enough line. The result is a softness to his work that I must overcome. It's all too "beautiful." Whereas I want something more harsh to contrast with the beauty, a starkness and awed sweep. . . .

Grau has done a marvelous job of turning what's innate in Schreck into the Nosferatu. Schreck's been bound into a three-quarter-length jacket, buttoned up tightly. His makeup (I must show his hands today) will take three hours.

ENDLESS DISCOVERIES. Water from a spring so pure the animals take the trough to be empty. The play of shadow off it in twilight like the marble ceilings of seaside hotels. Grau, in his other hat as producer, complains that we continue to fall behind our schedule. But what shots! Today an open cart-shed full of rakes and scythes, and that gray spider on the backlit orb-web. Broken sunlight through isinglass. Wagner's work, viewed each night, is breathtaking: in clarity, in richness of detail, in contour. One can find that same soft brilliance in certain kinds of silver polished with skins.

GRETA CAME to me with an idea for Heligoland: her character, Ellen, waiting for Hutter's return at a seaside graveyard—stark crosses at oblique and neglected attitudes on the dune, with the sea beyond. A wonderful idea: the natural world enlisted and compromised by the Nosferatu. The natural world operating under the shadow of the supernatural. Enormous tranquillity in the context of unease and dread: for whom is she waiting?

A discussion grows out of our enthusiasm. Endless polarities—west and east, good and evil, civilization and wilderness, reason and passion, with the contested terrain in every case the body of the woman. The obsession is not with the oppositions as much as the areas between them—the possibility that they're not such oppositions. Hence the connections between Hutter and the Nosferatu, Ellen and the Nosferatu.

The differences between the Self and the Other start to collapse. In Stoker's novel, the woman from the village sees Harker at the window and identifies *him* as the vampire: "Monster, give me my child!"

STILL NO Spiess. Lunched with Galeen and Greta in Poczamok. Bathed in the river. Raspberries!

THE PUBLICITY assistant back in Berlin sent Grau an article from the *Literarische Welt,* which he passed on to me: "Murnau has become a new kind of being who thinks directly in photographs.

Murnau is a kind of modern centaur: he and the camera joined to form a single body." An image lifted from Lasker-Schüler's image of me as "made of leaf and bark / Of early morn and centaur blood." The article ends by announcing that "Murnau teaches us to *see* the modern film; others will teach us to *feel* it."

STILL NO Spiess. The headaches back. The doctors unhappy with my kidneys. Great pain while urinating. The crew sits about and waits. At times I'm ashamed of their confidence. What have I achieved so far?

A single day left to do scenes that should take three or four, which is always how schedules evolve. Wagner points out that for the negative footage the vampire's carriage must be painted *white* so it will remain black. In the same way, Schreck must be clothed in white. Multiple disasters and new ideas make the last days on location a constant nightmare of clumsiness. Everyone falls over everyone else while the light slowly disappears. Four of us splash paint over the carriage in a fever. Grau fashions a white cloak out of a bedsheet. Eight in the morning becomes five in the afternoon.

IN THE night I dreamed of my father, the last time I saw him: on the platform of the Berlin railway station, standing amid the depressed and nondescript second-class passengers. I was leaning out the train window. For a moment we looked at each other; then the train moved off and he disappeared among the crowd. Then I was in a dead woman's apartment, gazing at the remains of an unappetizing meal, the head and bones of some smoked fish. A sort of ghost meal.

I lay awake afterwards, and scribbled down an idea for a general shot: Hutter looks around the room, which seems to him utterly changed. The damp wallpaper, the stains on the floor, the rough furniture, the depressing well of the courtyard beyond. All these things exude a rank physicality, a bleak reality, a hostility directed at him.

# INTERIORS

SPIESS IS gone. Frau Reger handed me his note a few minutes after I dropped my valise in the front hall. It was typed. Civilization, as I well knew, had become unbearable, and he'd decided to flee from it and build a new life in the South Seas, perhaps the Dutch East Indies.

A DAY off work. Unreturned calls to Lasker-Schüler and Veidt. The company puzzled. Wagner attributes it to exhaustion.

Doubts about the whole project. There is an essentially trivial quality at the heart of film's fascination—a nervous, aggressive vulgarity.

I'm surprised, too, by the intensity of my despondency at Spiess's departure. As he once wrote me, Hans *is your obsession. I'm just the Catamite who assists you in all your ceremonies of regret.*

LATE FOR work the next day. Unheard of for Murnau. An inspection of the interiors built by Grau and his assistants at the Jofa studios at Berlin-Johannisthal. More than a few ironies here: the largest film-production studio in Europe has taken shape on the grounds of the old Albatros-Werke. I make movies now where engineers made planes for Allmenröder and me.

It's a hard place to get used to, a huge dirigible-hangar of exposed steel girders and glass that makes all sound harsh and prone to echo. First check of the set of the castle dining hall. An arrangement like a child's playhouse in the middle of the vast space.

Grau was enraged by the way his sketches had been realized. He ranted, upbraided, drew new versions in the air, and tore down flats, while I stood by befuddled by his talent and passion. This is more often his production than mine, and in the face of my weakness he's the glue that holds everything together.

He disagreed about the layout of the great hall. He complained the scenic space gave the impression of being cut off by accident. I told him that the compositions were intended to seem part of a larger, organic effect; he said *No*, banging a table so that a plate jumped: the artistic decor ought to be the perfect composition at the center of which the action took place.

Wagner mediated, suggesting we weren't as far apart as we thought. I suggested a compromise: we do it my way. Grau left.

Wagner's steadiness is invaluable. I work beautifully with him, usually by anticipating him. I show him an inferior composition; he studies it despondently, then gets excited, begins fiddling, and in minutes produces exactly what we need.

When Grau returns, the three of us walk the set. I eliminate the chairs (too light and too modern) and allow the fireplace (which doesn't work). Wagner shows us where he wants the second camera. We make fun of his precision. Grau gets onto his hands and knees with a slide rule, and I shout "Closer! Farther! Closer!" while he moves it incrementally this way and that. Spiess had watched us do that in Czechoslovakia, and later said that we'd seemed a family he'd never be a part of.


OUTSIDE THE studio we wait irritably for taxis in the rain. Schreck leans against a wall in the darkness, his arms folded. He has no hat. Grau is staying at a nearby hotel. Wagner and I are going back to the Grunewald. Out of the darkness Schreck asks what we think a vampire is. Wagner says: Corpses who during their lifetime had been sorcerers, werewolves, people excommunicated by the Church, excommunicated from their lives: suicides, drunkards, heretics, apostates, and those cursed by their parents. Grau, after a pause, looks at me and says: Demons who dwell in the corpses of men, to instruct them in vice, and lead them to wickedness.

SOME CONVERSATIONS with Leo, Spiess's brother, about his possible whereabouts. Leo is unsympathetic. The Spiesses were a great Baltic family. Leo is Kapomeister at the Staatsoper Berlin. There's no guarantee he'll even let me know if he hears anything.

I BLAME Spiess as often as I blame myself for Hans. Yet with who else can I share this obsession? He liked to call me the administrator of my own inhibitions. He amended Hans's nickname and called me Bayard, the Knight Soaked in Reproach. He said we were both to blame, always with that air of knowing the price of everything.

THE SHOOTING begins and the wolfhound that was Galeen's idea refuses to film. He takes his place properly, but leaves as soon as the cameras begin to roll and returns when they're finished. We attempt the simple scene of Wangenheim in his room in the castle, a tiny whitewashed room with sharp angles and a huge, crib-like bed in the period style. He is to read from *The Book of Vampires* (*"THE NOSFERATU. From the bloody sins of mankind a creature will be born . . ."*) and go to the window, throwing it open to look into the starless night, while beyond his door in the depths of the castle the horror gathers. He swaggers through the motions, ruining everything. Multiple takes, two or three quiet conversations with him. The film is nearly always finished before one's had time to get the actors to forget the bad habit of "giving a performance."

Then, through the viewfinder, everything was too washed out. I begged Wagner to bring more contrast into the shot, so we set about dramatizing the light, hanging screens to define the space and throw shadows on the far walls. Then Wangenheim began botching the simple actions, dropping the book, catching his foot in the bedclothes. I hid myself, thinking him more likely to manage without me around. At last he made it without disaster to the window, but then it was Wagner's turn: the camera caught on its cable and didn't pan. Grau could stand it no longer, and left. We broke for five minutes and did it once more, with only an hour of time left, and miraculously, everything worked. Everyone relaxed. The scene fell together and even a cat wandered through as if it were at home.

At the end of each day, everything but the sets themselves is stowed away out of sight. The rights to *Dracula* have not been purchased and Grau has begun receiving inquisitive letters from solicitors representing Bram Stoker's wife.


TALKED TO Grau about Wangenheim's costume. Colors offer different sensibilities to light even in black-and-white photography. For the scenes in the castle, Wangenheim should have a blue waistcoat. This is not superstitious or fetishistic; it has to do with the value of gray that blue will provide.

Also: first day for Ruth Landshoff, who plays Ellen's sister. The daughter of the shipowner, not even a professional actress, but someone I noticed months ago in the Grunewald, on her way to school. Beautiful and refined, she reminded me of a picture by Kaulbach, and I went to great lengths to meet her mother and ask permission for her to take part in the filming during her holidays. I'm irresistibly drawn to the idea of *this* woman in my film, in this infernal vision of swarming rats, of pestilential boats, of men who suck blood, of dark vaults, of black carriages pulled by phantom horses. . . .

During a half day's shooting, she stands beside me, not sure where else to go. Wangenheim flirts with her. Wagner and I are filming Ellen's sleep-connection to the vampire. The only sounds are the turning of the camera and Wangenheim's whispering. It's customary to build additional sets while shooting's going on, a crowd of people standing nearby giving orders at the tops of their voices. But I work in silence, the silence of the film itself. A journalist from my parents' hometown compared work on my set to a memorial service, presided over by "a tall thin gentleman in his white work coat, standing a bit out of the way, issuing directions in a very low voice."

I DON'T understand how it is that this generation has not seen the rise of a true poet of film. For all the arts, one is able to cite great masters born to understand them exceptionally. There should come geniuses of the screen who know instinctively what it alone has the power to do. At the moment, we found our stories on novels, stage plays, etc. In the future, we'll think film and dream film.

MORE TELEPHONE calls to Leo Spiess. He's taken to hanging up on me.

.   .   .

WAGNER TOOK me aside with doubts about Wangenheim's performance. Wangenheim's aggressive terror, he said, inhibited his own. The hero, presented to us as bold/hardy/audacious/daring/venturesome and plucky, suddenly passes from all that to convulsive terror? I thanked him and reminded him it was too late to replace Wangenheim. His was not a comment timed to fill me with confidence.

FOR THE vampire's arrival: lack of movement makes the eye impatient. *Use such impatience.*

FILMED GRANACH, as Knock, the house agent under the sway of the Nosferatu. A relief working with an old friend. During breaks he told the crew how as students of Reinhardt's we'd lie on the floor of the stage-box to hear and see him work with actors (he allowed no one to view his rehearsals). The scene came off perfectly. Reading the cabalistic letter sent by the vampire, Granach seems dropped in from another world, his spindly hunchback shifting and jerking, his ugly smile making sense of the strange symbols. A last touch was all his: raising his head upon finishing, as if greeting the evil. Wonderfully disturbing sense of the diabolism closer to home.

The happy accidents of art. As the Austrians say, *Es ist passiert*—It just happened like that.

REMINDER TO the labs: the lettering of the titles should be lanky and tortuous, like that of *Caligari*. The background, a poisonous green. A tooth is giving me great pain.

.  .  .

IN CZECHOSLOVAKIA, Spiess related to me a dream that he was Ellen in the film. He went up to the bedroom before his husband. At the side of the bed he heard the fluttering of a bird. The air was disturbed. He didn't light the lamp or draw the curtain. The streetlight provided the only light. He couldn't keep awake. In a park nearby, the wind moved the trees. It was as if he'd been chloroformed.

Even after his departure, he continues to provide information on the lore of the vampire. Alone in my room, unable to sleep, I go over, in his handwriting, the last three stages of the etymological history of the word: the Old Church Slavonic for "fugitive," the early Common Slavic for "the one who drinks in," and the later Slavic for "neighbor."

FIRST INTERIOR shooting of Schreck as the Nosferatu. Made up, he wanders the dining hall set in preparation, and the stonework, windows, and doors come to life. It's we, ridiculous ghosts, in our modern clothes, who look like intruders. The scene of his dinner with Hutter: the hall through the camera appearing to have gigantic dimensions. In the center a massive Renaissance table. In the distance the huge fireplace. The Nosferatu reading Hutter's letter of introduction: sharp ratlike teeth over the lower lip. His eyes, over the top margin of the letter, as he hears the clock strike midnight. A snake hypnotizing its victim. Wangenheim smart enough to stop acting as the drama reaches its height, understanding the audience will have already reached the required degree of tension. Afterwards some "executives" from Prana, friends of Grau's, in for lunch. A strange meal. Schreck, still made up as the Nosferatu, set his teeth on the table like part of the place-setting while he ate his soup.

.  .  .

THE PACE picks up. It must. One set is struck and another built in its place while Grau and Galeen and I confer with the actors for the day's next scene. More kidney trouble has thrown us a week behind. Grau called me at the Bühlershöh sanatorium to remind me that shooting had to be finished in four weeks, by 1 November. Some sets I'd asked him to save had been struck, he added, and I had to work more sensibly and avoid unnecessary takes. Film stock already cost thirty marks a meter, and no more would be forthcoming. Even with the help of the big banks, inflation was making it impossible to raise money. Agnuzzo, apparently, was tapped out.

TWELVE-HOUR DAYS. Many of us are fighting sunstroke caused by the arcs. Crew members rub raw grated potato on their faces to combat the burn. The Nosferatu greeting Hutter as it emerges from the darkness of the castle archway. Wagner suggests we use magnesium flares with the arcs to increase the effect of moonlight. Take after take. Schreck sweats and suffers under his makeup, and his forehead looks as if it's been varnished.

Everyone thinking about future commitments: Granach going back to the stage; Grau soon to begin scouting exteriors for Prana's next film. Wagner working with Lang. Galeen to direct his own *Stadt in Sicht*. We're all progressively losing the sense that we're held within the same dream—each of us beginning to wake up.

MY TROUBLE is naïveté. What I should do is overnumber the shots so the script girl could note increasing numbers accomplished each day, and Grau and Dieckmann would be steadily mollified.

Tensions continue with Grau over the schedule, our plans for the film, everything. As we get closer to the end, more and more of his energy goes into promotion and distribution, which is necessary but seems premature. After he's interviewed by *Der Film*, I have to read: "Each scene is given over to the director only when ready to be filmed; beforehand the artistic director has prepared it down to the smallest details, according to psychological and pictorial principles, and has sketched it out on paper. Each gesture, each costume (the era of 1840, approximately) and movement has been laid out with scientific rigor and calculated to produce a specific effect upon the spectator."

The publicity material is modeled on that old Expressionist hysteria. One of the handouts:

*Nosferatu was there. In the streets. Mongrels howled it. Babies cried it. Crooked branches traced its letters in the earth. The wind swept the word and carried it away, and dead leaves from the trees read "Nosferatu." It invaded everything. One could see it along walls, above streetlamps, in the eyes of those late to bed. It fastened to ganglia and sounded in bones. It clamored. It uttered cries like rats in a coffin. Maidens whispered it in their sleep. Above them in the darkness it formed, livid and ghastly pale, leaden and yellow, full of sulphur and fatal breath. And you? Do you still feel nothing? Nos-fer-a-tu—Nosferatu—beware.*

SHOT BY shot I know my way through. I will not give in until I have what I want. But every morning there we are, still on the set, with its dismal fraudulence, its flapping wall, and plaster gargoyles. Again I'll get worked up, pull my hair, go back to my room, start over.

Determined to do ten shots today, despite Wagner's pace, Grau's complaints, and the arcs, which keep fusing. Horrible quarrel. Wagner's taken to calling me the Schoolmaster.

FRUITLESS CHECK of steamship offices about Spiess. Found a gift he'd brought me at a dinner I'd arranged in my room in

Czechoslovakia. An erotic drawing of two boys and a man. We'd been tense and awkward. Wangenheim had wandered by while I was examining the drawing. The whole thing a Feydeau farce. Spiess had become distracted and impatient; in return, I was exhausted and short-tempered. He left before dessert.

A TELEGRAM back from Meidner. No help about Hans. His response was full of questions.

THE FIRST stalking of Hutter. Discussions with Wangenheim beforehand. What matters is not what the actors show me but what they hide. Above all, *what they don't suspect is in them.* I cite for him the Baroness in *Schloss Vogelöd*, who after her husband fends off her kiss and announces his renunciation of everything worldly, whispers distractedly to herself, "I'm longing for evil—seeing evil—wanting evil."

We begin. The set deathly quiet. Hutter in his room in the castle, huddled behind the door. He opens it a crack. View deep into dining hall. By the fireplace the Nosferatu, motionless, arms down, confrontationally stark against the background. Horrible lack of movement. Hutter supports himself on the doorpost. Terrible realizations dawning. Shut the door, shut it quickly! No bolt. No lock. He rushes to the window. (View of the forest at night: undergrowth; wolves raising their heads, howling.) The contrast between Hutter's movements and the Nosferatu's: frenzied panic vs. the terrible evenness of the advance. Hutter on his knees by the side of the bed. Stares at the door, which opens to half its width; then fully. Superimpositions of progressively closer shots of the vampire produce movement without movement, the figure swelling within the frame, the mechanism of nightmare. Wagner has the genius idea of having the figure penetrate a powerful light emanating from the side just as he enters the doorway. Four days of work.

TWO WEEKS left. Hardly eating. The same woman journalist from *Der Film* who interviewed Grau told me today that my face was like two profiles stuck together. Ellen's room, her decision to sacrifice herself, the final approach of the vampire are all still left to do. Two days of work on Ellen reading *The Book of Vampires*, until my temples are throbbing, my cheeks burning, my whole frame shivering. A few hours in my room drinking hot soup, contemplating the mistakes I made by plunging on at such a pace; but besides the lack of time, I feel myself fighting to prevent any kind of indecision at this point from demoralizing the unit.

My headaches worse. My kidneys breaking down. Berliners are tactless and cruel. On a bus yesterday a young lieutenant seated me with a flourish. The spectacle of this disintegrating thirty-three-year-old seems to make people laugh.

TAKE AFTER take of Ellen at the window, seeing the Nosferatu. She is at once pure (and therefore appalled by what she has to do) and impure (since she makes her bed available to the vampire). Greta not up to it. Wagner works with the inhumanity of all cameramen; he calibrates the lights at his own pace without noticing that Greta all that time is swaying on her feet. Grau looks on, his arms folded. The nerve storm finally breaks and she collapses. Wangenheim comforts her while we wait. The shooting goes far into the night.

THIS FEAR of coming to a standstill, of not being able to go on, of having to break off—it's connected to all of my other undertakings: loving, observing, participating. Everything, in short, that has called for perseverance.

LITTLE SLEEP; endless, crushing headaches. Granite pieces breaking behind my eyes. Cold sweat, palpitations, exhaustion. A full day without working at all. Grau in a frenzy of rage and despair over this preview, in a Marxist rag: "This occultism, which has victimized thousands of shaken minds since the war, is a strategy mounted by the industrial world to deflect the worker from his own political interests. Today the occult takes the place of religions that no longer attract clients. Workers! On your guard! Don't give your pennies to a spectacle designed to stupefy! Let the phantom 'Nosferatu' be devoured by his own rats!"

Grau's response? Ever more publicity. Prana has now spent more on publicity than on the film itself. It seems clearer and clearer to me that the whole enterprise is an enormous bluff. Where is the publicity money to come from? The Otto Riede Bank, according to Grau, but Wagner tells me this bank doesn't exist, and that Otto Riede is a simple employee. Yet the madness goes on. Grau plans a party on the release date: Saturday, March 4, "Prana's Day." He's secured the marble entry hall of the zoo, and commissioned a prologue by Kurt Alexander inspired by the introduction from Goethe's *Faust*. He's hired Elisabeth Grube of the national opera to perform with the ballet troupe. For musical accompaniment there will be the great harmonium "Dominator," transported to the site at massive cost. And all of this, he announces, will be filmed!

HOBBLED BACK to the set this morning accompanied by a nurse. Disoriented by the medication and exhaustion and worried all day by an oppressive sense that I'm out of touch with the world. Stagehands stood around in groups as if at union meetings, eyeing me. The whole film seemed moribund. Woke that night from dreams which moved like dirty water forming monstrous waves. Neck hurt.

AND THEN a late-afternoon wait in a pub across the street from the studio. Another problem with the arc lights. Wagner and I share wine, bread and butter, minced pork. I confess my fears, my inability to understand what I'm doing, to go on. Wagner tells me that I alone can do this. Seeing my face, he puts his hand to my cheek, in full view of the entire pub. That easily, his palm brings me a temporary peace. He's been viewing the footage, he tells me, and it's everything I've hoped for. He is such a mysterious figure, finally: cheerless and sober and intent on something outside my view.

A FEW hours' sleep. A breathing spell. The final sequence to be done, the Nosferatu's approach to Ellen.

The horror coming slowly, tensed like a predatory animal. A new idea of Grau's, necessitating a new set at this late date: nothing but the shadow of Nosferatu on the wall of the stairs, mounting with dreadful slowness, then more quickly, an awful quick-footed walk, fingernails dripping, until it pauses beside the door. The hand and fingers extending elastically along the wall. In the room Ellen shrinks before the monster we still don't see, except for the black shadow of his hand spreading across her white body like ink. She jerks her head down in anticipation of his touch, as her husband had. The shadow fist seizes her heart. And then in the darkness, on the very side of the frame, obscenely unobtrusive, the Nosferatu feeding.

THE SHOOTING done. A week's rest. The unit comes back together one last time to view the rough projection before the final cutting begins. Grau, Wagner, Galeen, Wangenheim, Greta—all of this is now a memory to them, like a party they found puzzling and absorbing but not pleasant.

Galeen torments me with an article in the *Berliner Tageblatt*, reading for the group: "Of all the film directors, Murnau is the most German. A Westphalian, reserved, severe on himself, severe on others, severe for the cause. Outwardly grim, never envious, always alone, his successes and failures arising from the same source, each of his works complete, authentic, direct, logical, cold, harsh, and absolute, like Gothic art." Much hooting. Grau suggests it sounds like an obituary.

We view what we have. Some pleasures—the opportunity to render fluid human time, so painful in its rigidity, to arrange and rearrange it, our small triumph over the inexorable. Again struck by how often the camera could see what I couldn't feel. In that negative footage of the vampire's carriage driving through a white forest, ground mist that we barely noticed during the shooting has photographed *black*. Drifting along before the horses' onrushing hooves, a ghost smoke or dream-vapor, like pestilence itself.

Long stretches of footage so bad no one will comment. Enduring them, I begin to tell myself I can still do what I set out to achieve; yet the faults in the work are mine alone.

In the darkness, Spiess's absence is more comfortable and familiar. The more he pursued me, the more I restrained my passion for him. This sense of never being at home, with anyone, grows stronger the older I get.

More footage. My concentration dissipates. I remember living in a series of hotels, when I was very small, before Father bought the estate. One small old hotel in particular, by the sea, a little room full of sun in which you could smell the apples and the waves.

Someone yawns. Another shifts in his chair. In the silence of a

changeover in reels, I can hear us all—Grau, Wagner, Greta—
murmuring with pleasure and amusement. Behind the whirring
of Wagner cueing up the final leader, we can hear the sound of
many voices singing in the garden below: children outside our
dark little room, shouting in the sunlight.

# DER LETZTE MANN

5/3/24 . A few weeks ago I found the notebooks from my first film projects, optimistically marked *Murnau—Film 1919*. The first entries involved *Satanas*, untitled at that point. They were instructions to myself, to convince myself of my own authority, in a loose-leafed binder that probably did the opposite for my young crew. I was touched, leafing back through them.

*Master precision. Be a precision instrument yourself.*

*Problem: to make what you see be seen, through the intermediary of a machine that does not see as you do. To make what you understand be understood, through the intermediary of that same machine.*

*Rid yourself of accumulated untruths. Know your own resources. You are not "directing" someone else, but yourself.*

A few weeks after those words were written, a Tarzan-film out of America crystallized my sense that in terms of the arts, I was moving into a new world. This Tarzan-film set itself with sovereign blitheness above probability, truthfulness, logic, and other such modest criteria of modern thought. But the electrifying thing was that *I did not notice those flaws as long as the film was showing;* I only became aware of the inner incoherence on the way home, when I stopped at a café and tried to rework what I'd seen. Then I confronted closed doors and absurd coincidences. But even so, I felt no anger or betrayal, and smiled. For despite its absurdity, the Tarzan-film was a masterpiece of modern technique: suspenseful, adventurous, and high-spirited. Instead of intellectual gratification, it had captivated and delighted its audience with technical finesse.

My life changed there in that café. The insight that even discriminating viewers could be seduced by such an approach was exhilarating: I realized the kinetic character of cinema, the primacy of pictorial rhythm. Understandings that I'd come to during the war concerning the ways photography could *move* had been given a form.

Since I've had the power to choose, I've worked with Karl Freund or Fritz Arno Wagner as cameramen for that reason: they see the camera as an artistic element in and of itself, and understand that it cannot, in its present immobility, express the potential of cinematography. The old practice dictates a static composition as the backdrop before which the actors cavort: only the space within the reach of a shackled apparatus.

Some of us—Freund, Wagner, and Carl Mayer, who's working on the screenplay—want a variable, multiple, living scene. We intend to shatter the bonds that keep the audience as passive as the theatergoer in his seat; we intend to give the spectator the illusion of *agency*. Theatrical space will be left behind. The camera will travel through uncharted territory. Filmmaking will seem to have come from somewhere else, and not from the human hand.

Years ago this seemed even farther from realization. Every so often I'd discover in the trade papers someone who shared my obsession. When Hermann Warm declared in an interview, "The cinema must be a *living* sketch," I hired him as set designer for *Schloss Vogelöd*. When Carl Theodor Dreyer, lecturing in Berlin, spoke of the camera as an active part of "the music of images," I wrote to him and asked to pick his brain. I saved everything from the practical to the inspirational in a file, then new, slender, and clean; now old, bulging, and weather-stained.

I'm convinced that this is the point at which my will meets and moves with destiny, as if life, as the poet said, was a horse, to whose motion one yielded only after having trained the animal to the utmost. All of my work in theater and film has been leading up to this: the unchained camera.

. . .

WE'VE COME together—Freund, Mayer, and myself—to realize
our ambition. We have the talent and the budget of which we've
dreamed. We have no more excuses.

The film is to be called *Der Letzte Mann*—from the biblical
admonition that the last will be first—and concerns the tragicom-
edy of a hotel doorman, proud of his braided livery, admired by
his family and neighbors, the general of his own back courtyard.
Too old to carry the heavy luggage, he's retired to the gentlemen's
lavatories, forced to exchange his uniform for a simple white
jacket. His family feels dishonored, and he becomes the laughing-
stock of the neighbors, who take their revenge for the adulation
they had lavished upon him.

It's a pre-eminently German tragedy. It can only be understood in a country where uniform is King. The old morality based
on Wilhelmine authority is pitted against this new matter-of-
factness that trusts only money. The thought of the film is this:
they take away his uniform from a man, and what has he lost?
With his uniform he can be king, general, judge, with all the
power of his position. Take that away, and what remains?

The idea was Mayer's. A newspaper report about a toilet
attendant's suicide had prompted him to write the story. Originally it was to be directed by Lupu Pick, as part of a triptych,
with *Scherben* and *Sylvester* as the flanking panels; the protagonist
was to be played by Pick himself. A disagreement put an end to
the plan, and Pommer assigned the script to me at Jannings's suggestion. Then he granted the project a budget *three times* higher
than we'd submitted. Why? The appeal of the American market.
The size of their exhibition circuit. But also in retaliation for Hollywood's invasion of our market. Anyway, this was the thinking
behind the millions thrown at Lang for his *Die Nibelungen*. Ufa is
staking its existence on cracking the American market. Pommer's

program will cost too much to recoup itself in Germany alone.

Of the one million six hundred thousand marks set aside, Jannings is pocketing six hundred thousand. Most of the rest is funding an arena for formal experiment.

This is fine with Pommer; if the film doesn't represent something exciting and different, then why on earth would the Americans buy it? Especially given that the story is one that a non-German mind will have trouble comprehending as any kind of tragedy at all. As Pommer put it in his closing remarks at our first preproduction meeting: "Please invent something new, even if it's crazy!"

OUR PLAN is simple. The whole script has been modified to be based on the continuous movement of the camera.

Mayer toyed with the notion in his script for *Sylvester*, but Pick did little with it. For the dramatic shot of the clock just before midnight, Pick and Seeber, his cameraman, constructed a two-level platform with wheels, a huge thing that looked like one of the old Farman bombers stripped of its wings, though they never took it any further: the camera could now slowly close in on an object. Could it turn? Climb? Descend? Swoop?

Those questions obsess Mayer as much as the rest of us. His scripts are dramatic poems—a detailed narration of the shots and pacing, the film imagined in verse. For him the camera is not just a helpful optical device but an extension of his senses. He tests each shot he imagines with a viewfinder Freund gave him; such is his persistence to comprehend more about what we're doing. Late at night he appears at my house, a squat man with a vaguely Oriental face, waiting impatiently for the door to be opened so that we might resume our discussion. He works day and night. He takes such long walks to sort things out that his neighbors call him the Mailman.

His writing has prompted both his critics and colleagues to view the art form's capabilities with greater precision. With his script, we're halfway there; we need only determine how to pull off the miracles envisioned. The script pages for the scene in which the doorman steals back the uniform of which he's been stripped:

*FADE IN: The front of the hotel at night.*
*CLOSE-UP: feeling his way through the revolving door: the old man.*
*In his hands, the uniform.*
*He listens behind him, like a wary thief.*
*But suddenly . . . what's that?*
*Light flashes from a lantern.*
*It's swaying in the wind,*
*while now the old man gets ready to run. And . . .*
*WHILE THE CAMERA RUNS IN FRONT OF HIM,*
*He starts convulsively squeezing the uniform. And . . .*
*SINCE THE CAMERA IS MOVING MORE QUICKLY THAN HIM:*
*Soon he's silhouetted against the hotel.*
*STILL MOVING, THE CAMERA RETURNS TO HIS FACE.*
*Does his stained conscience rule him?*
*And now! What fear!*
*The hotel! Growing and growing, larger and larger!*
*And while he's now running, panting—*
*Do tentacles stretch out behind him?*
*Will they want to overwhelm him?*
*Here his knees give out,*
*And he falls against a wall.*
*HERE THE CAMERA CATCHES UP WITH HIM.*
*LONG-SHOT: The hotel in darkness.*
*LS: Here he remains.*
*Panting horribly.*
*He squeezes the uniform against his chest.*

*What had he seen back there?*
*What in the bulk of the hotel had threatened him?*
*WE SEE FROM HIS POINT OF VIEW:*
*The hotel.*
*It stands there serenely, in the peace of the night. And now,*
*LS: The Old Man*
*Still gazing in that direction.*
*Ever panting.*
*And then, what's this?*
*It's a guffaw, or a cackle!*
*Is he completely crazy?*
*Anyway, he has the uniform!*
*He even has the cap, which he puts on.*
*Now he gets into his overcoat. Adjusts it.*
*All the same, he still pants.*
*He finally relaxes,*
*And now, stroking his beard, smoothing it,*
*He is once again the Doorman.*
*And meanwhile . . .*
*THE FRAME FADES QUICKLY TO BLACK.*

I work away from the quiet stasis of my study, in the cafés bordering the Grunewald. I sit at outdoor tables surrounded by chaos and take notes in English, which provides a soothing sense of privacy that the noisy talk can't disturb. I drink milk from tall narrow glasses that don't stay cold. During breaks, I consider the red freckles on the backs of my hands. My spine and eyes ache. The time is impossible to determine. The chestnut shadows wheel across the gravel. I organize my notecards into piles by category, leave money on the plate, and meander home, thinking, This is what freedom is. This is how I should always have lived.

.   .   .

EVERY SATURDAY, a visit, alone, to the circus. Hans's ponies. I feed them carrots during intermissions. A day or two of immobility afterwards; listless work or none at all.

THIS IS MY film, too. The psychic violence in it is mine. All my films demonstrate that we create violence out of our memories and not out of what is presented to our vision, just the way in childhood we fill the blanks of our understanding with image-stories we manufacture in retrospect.

THE SUBTLE power struggle with Jannings has already begun. He's concerned about playing second fiddle to the technicians. He also wants to make certain of my gratitude. He wants me properly cowed. He dropped by my office after a makeup check to chat. He said he thought the film's main question to be "What makes a man a man?" He remarked on the humor of a homosexual making a film entitled *The Last Man.*

HERE IT'S 1924 and Ufa still has no effects department. The American example remains to be emulated. In the meantime the creation of special-effects or trick photography—all innovation, of any sort, with the camera—is left to on-the-spot resourcefulness and improvisation. The basis of problem-solving is not systematic research but chance and inspiration.

For that, Freund is ideal. He knows more about the technical side of filmmaking than anyone on Earth. He was in the business in 1906 as a fifteen-year-old projectionist. A master of the established procedures, he never hesitates when innovations are proposed, and proposes most of them himself. He has an army of assistants, each filled with fear and devotion.

One he sat on before firing. He's a fat man, so fat he had to be released from the Army after only three months in 1915. His weight doesn't hinder his manipulation of the cameras, though the vest buttons under his white work-coat may be straining and popping. He has two all-consuming interests: the science of camerawork and the safety and virtue of his teenaged daughter.

His working habits are as ordered as his equipment. During a break once, I watched him take a delicate shutter apart. This was of special interest to me because, as a young man, I too had taken a shutter apart, and knew what to expect. I had removed the screws from the front and lifted off the top, whereupon the entire internal economy of the shutter exploded in my face and scattered across the floor.

Working with watchmaker's screwdrivers, he removed the screws one by one, placing each in a row on a sheet of clean paper, the edges of which were folded up. The first screw he placed in the upper left corner, and each subsequent piece followed in a line from left to right in the order of its removal. Then he eased the front of the case loose like someone lifting a foreign object from a lover's eye. All the springs stayed in place beneath. He removed them with fine-pointed pliers. Then came the blades of the iris diaphragm, one after another. At every moment, he lingered where I would have rushed.

It'll be his duty throughout this project to rein in my impatience in the same way.

Our watchword will be simplicity, achieved through the fullest possible realization of our technical resources. Our ambition is to photograph thought.

PRINCIPAL TECHNICAL work at the studio began yesterday. I announced the time for the next day's organizational meeting and pep talk as six a.m. It seemed to fit the overall fanaticism of the company. The assembled stagehands answered in one voice, *"Jawohl!"*

AFTER DINNER, a walk in the park to clear my head. Sandri accompanied me.

The police have taken notice of my preference for exotic young house-servants. Sandri is an especially intriguing Malaysian. Each house-servant lasts only a few months before he aches to return home, wherever that might be—Borneo, Java, the Solomons. I pay their way. In the meantime, they build up a savings to take back with them. Many have families.

There have been awkwardnesses. Frau Reger has been rigid with disapproval since this practice started. But she runs the household and her loyalty is firm. She hasn't offered her resignation, and I haven't requested it.

Last night I found him looking through these journals. He was stretched out in my morning robe across my bed, paging around. Later I found in the margins next to some of my sketches peculiar patterns of lines and circles.

The city still frightens him. When we have time together, he wishes to visit the park. He likes to inspect new areas and follow different paths, which in the Grunewald is not difficult. We periodically pass the Morals Police, who devote a sizeable part of their force to the city parks. They travel in pairs, lingering by shadowy thickets or resting amiably on benches. They're instructed to proceed with the greatest circumspection, since for them "a hundred omissions are preferable to a single error" in terms of accusations.

Nevertheless, there's always a tremor when they fall into step behind us.

When we went by car to the Friedrichstrasse to buy a new hall carpet, he was fascinated with the prostitutes. I was astonished at the speed with which he recognized them; I'm never really sure.

The odd restraint of the Berlin prostitute creates a tension of *not knowing* which itself is perversely exciting. The slow walk alongside, the willingness to catch one's eye, and yet the seeming lack of interest: perhaps that young girl is only window-shopping? The siren with carmine lips and Egyptian eyes turns out to be a mother with three in tow; the sprite from a children's book turns out to be soliciting. After the war some of the younger prostitutes wore widows' veils, and refused to stay in certain districts, so that everywhere the streets were suffused with a pervasive erotic ambiguity.

I BEGAN my habit of house-servants five months to the day after Spiess's departure. Soon after that, Lasker-Schüler asked how I dealt with the paradox of that sort of behavior and my supposed ongoing feelings for Hans. They were not, I told her, the same thing.

Yet the day she asked, I was up all night reliving what I'd done to Hans. The next morning, I arranged for the return voyage of the house-servant of the moment, a boy from Borneo.

SANDRI HAS taken to leaving the house less and less. Recently he's had to be cajoled even to walk in the park. He refuses all fish and now eats only fruit, the rinds and seeds of which he leaves scattered around the house.

Most of the time he sits by the gramophone, which he reveres, playing over and over again a record from America that fascinates him: "The Vamp of Savannah."

I'm of two minds about this. He's erratic enough that his presence in public generates anxiety. He accompanied me to meet a Swiss camera-manufacturer at a nearby hotel, and was instructed to wait near the front desk. After my business, I discovered that

Sandri had been put out on the street. The hotel detective said that he'd noticed in the lobby what he'd considered to be a pervert. He wondered if a beating administered by the night manager in the garden out back would be appropriate. I said that if he made it his duty to beat house-servants, I would make it mine to see him off to Brandenburg for five years. He was unfazed. I returned home shaken. Sandri, too, was out of sorts.

OUR SECOND day at the studio. Eighteen minutes by car. The new driver is sour and not good-looking. The occasional fond thought for Huber, now off with the Freikorps harassing the French occupation troops in the Ruhr.

The Freikorps: what wicked fairy placed *that* gift in our cradle?

The approach to the studios in Neubabelsberg has a depressing aspect even on a sunny morning. The carpenters' and costumers' shops, the great hall: everything seems temporary and messily utilitarian, scattered across weedy and empty lots. Trash heaps and temporary storage piles surround the buildings. Memories of that wilderness of railway tracks and Hans's kiss. In the distance, scrubby pines eventually give way to Potsdam.

On the next lot they're filming *Zur Chronik von Grieshuus*. Fifty or so day-hires toil on a fortress wall, slopping its facade with mortar. The car drops me at my office opposite the carpenters' shops, so my day can begin with the endless noise of saws, and the clunk and thunk of wood thrown about.

The office is dark, with one small window. On the back wall I've hung a Chinese tapestry in blue and gold of a brooding spirit spied upon by two heraldic beasts. I spend the entire morning fussing around my workspace, cleaning up. Once I can see my table and chair and desk, I'm open for business.

.    .    .

THE FIRST meeting of the day is with Mayer, about script changes. He wants the camera to close in rapidly on the buttons of the doorman's coat at the moment the uniform is stripped off. That seems to me a good example of a moment when the camera should *not* be moving. He's constantly egging on the metaphysical meaning of every object. The doorman's umbrella is his sceptre; the stripped buttons, a pseudo-military degradation; the revolving door, the whirlpool of life. To couple such objects with camera movement is to make them all the more ham-handed.

He's sure to argue about this. His images are about intensity, not subtlety.

His childhood was a chapter from a Dickens novel. He was born in Graz, a Jew, the son of a man obsessed with gambling. When he was sixteen, his father, after losing a bet, asked the children to stand in the street and then killed himself. Mayer alone was responsible for his three brothers. During the day, he fixed barometers and advertised for an optician on street corners; at night he was an extra in peasant theaters and sang in choirs in Linz. He brought his brothers to Germany, seeking greater opportunity, and, during the early months of the war, earned a living drawing Hindenburg's portrait on postcards in coffeehouses.

He spent the war years in a desperate battle with military psychiatrists. He was a pacifist. To avoid prison, he needed to prove himself mentally deranged. He would not become a soldier, not only because he refused to see his brothers sent to an orphanage but also because he refused to learn the "craftsmanship of murder," as he put it. He was unabashed about speaking that way around veterans. For a while after we met, he called me the Flying Ace.

He said he refused to kill for a Fatherland gone mad. Apparently, his psychiatrist even tried hypnosis, under which he made Mayer repeat phrases like "I *can* kill." The psychiatrist became the model for Dr. Caligari.

Mayer and Janowitz, his Czech friend, wrote *Caligari* in the winter of 1919 in Berlin, during the last days of the revolution. They were oppressed by the Molochs running the munitions factories, the icy "turnip winter," the casualty notices in the newspapers. Their haunt, like mine, became the amusement park in the Kantstrasse, where the sideshows were so appalling that one couldn't wrench one's eyes from them. Horrible lusts were abroad. Hunger and misery festooned with electric lights and mechanical music. Adolescent girls tracked by sad-eyed shopkeepers wearing their one good suit, and occasionally lured into hansom cabs.

Like me, they found themselves drawn to the place after activities had ceased for the night, when only the romantically inclined and the sinister remained in the darkness under the scaffoldings of the rides. Black shadows stained our faces.

There, one night, they came across an attraction who seemed to be performing whether the fair was open or not—a man under a sign in huge letters that read MAN OR MACHINE? who, with dead eyes, in a seeming stupor, was tearing links off a chain and bending metal bars, while his "handler," or hypnotist, looked on as if the show were just for him. Then and there, according to Mayer, the story of Caligari and Cesare was conceived.

They both write very imagistically. Mayer calls it "brain-photography."

How good were Erich Pommer's instincts? Janowitz and Mayer read him the entire weird and unprecedented script at four in the afternoon, and he'd paid for it by eight that same evening. That night the two writers dined in solitary splendor in the vast and empty dining room of the Hotel Hessler. Many courses, and an old Burgundy. The next morning they retrieved their most important valuables from the local pawnbrokers. And Pommer had in his hands the blueprint for the biggest international hit this industry has ever produced.

·   ·   ·

DESPITE KNOWING just about everyone on-screen, we were completely taken in, watching the thing. The usual world of smirking dolls with bared teeth and oxlike eyes was gone. With *Caligari,* the artist had slipped into that crude phantasmagoria and had begun to create. Space had been given a voice.

FOR MAYER and Janowitz, the script had to be a straitjacket for the director, tight, precise, and balanced, with strong belts and fasteners, so that nothing could escape from their instructions. Mayer still writes that way. Each change I consider causes other parts of the structure to unexpectedly totter.

WHILE I'M still waiting for Mayer, I'm summoned by telephone to the great hall to adjudicate a dispute between Freund and the set designers, Herlth and Röhrig. Eight in the morning and they're already an hour into their argument.

The four main city sets are already half finished. The hall is a tangle of scaffold towers and cranes, shouts and hammering. On one set the model skyscrapers that the doorman will view from his post are over seventeen meters high. I gape at them like a tourist. Behind them we've built a large asphalt expanse of cars and street signs, life-sized in the foreground and smaller as they recede, so that by the last row they're only a foot tall. From the front there's the undeniable impression of being in a plaza of great dimensions.

At the base of a skyscraper, both sides give an impassioned version of their case while I wait like a referee at a football match. Freund claims that their perspective in depth will flatten out through the viewfinder. Herlth and Röhrig claim to have taken that into account by exaggerating the relief on the models' facades. Both sides attempt to cow me with the free use of technical specifications.

Herlth argues with the intensity of a zealot. He believes a production company should have the messianic fervor of a medieval cathedral-builders' guild, with the film architect as the *spiritus rector*, the intellectual and artistic leader for his colleagues.

I decide in favor of Freund, since what's paramount is what the camera sees, and on that he's the ultimate authority. Herlth is devastated. Röhrig throws up his hands and calls the carpenters down from the scaffolds.

Back at my office, Mayer raises no protest at my suggestion about the buttons. He's fixed on some other part of the scenario; if the idea works out, he'll discuss it with me. He leaves like the somnambulist who made him famous.

It seems prudent to use the unscheduled free time to smooth ruffled feathers, so I return to the great hall. Herlth is nowhere to be found. When he returns, he will devote himself to his slide rule at the design studio, working out the changes.

Röhrig is completing the miniature elevated train on the adjacent set. He sees me approach. He has a sloping forehead and a sullen, apprehensive aspect, and always seems to have been badly shaven. He looks like a convict. His partner is Italian-looking, with a high forehead and wavy black hair, like a second-rate seducer of matrons from Capri. Herlth does the designing, Röhrig the building. They consider everyone to be implacably in league against them, and, feeling endlessly put-upon, they do superb work. Of the two, Herlth is easier to deal with. I watch Röhrig for a while before I'm moved to pitch in and help.

The train will only be a foot or so high. The camera mark is inches from the point where it will pass. Röhrig is busy working on litter and weeds for the roadbed—cloth fibers, glass wool, and tiny bits of paper, hand painted. The trestle is plywood, with small wooden buttons for rivets. Black paint mixed with graphite approximates the metallic sheen of iron.

I'm a little boy again. We work in silence. Röhrig occasionally gestures as to where he wants something to go. I'm reminded of something Herlth said: that this work is a kind of intoxication for me, an enchantment with *process* that's familiar only to the research scientist or the surgeon during an operation. I spend twenty minutes I could have spent more profitably elsewhere on my hands and knees beside a Lilliputian crossing signal. If my brothers could see this: our little theaters in Wilhelmshöhe come again to life. Röhrig maintains his silence but in his own way seems pleased by my attention. Herlth returns with sketches and his figures-notebook and draws him back to the more pressing problem of the skyscrapers. Their crew slowly assembles around them. I give up on the miniature weeds, my hands spotted with sticky glue and fibers.

BY THE camera shed, I have to negotiate the set of the back steps leading to the doorman's apartment. The steps are more suitable to a line of heralds than a petit-bourgeois back garden. What are they thinking? In a pocket notebook I write, as I walk, *Steps——???*

BESIDE THE shed is the field lined with parked cars and carts. Every so often, small boys are chased away halfheartedly by the retired policeman hired to oversee the lot.

Inside it's badly ventilated. Some idiot has painted the corrugated roof black. Though large fans are blowing, everyone's sweating like a horse anyway. Freund and his assistants are working on what looks like a child's slide. All the exhausting preparatory work, without which the true work would be impossible! The camera operator is to sit on a greased wooden platform inside the slide. One of the assistants is testing it with a camera that's long since been cannibalized for spare parts. Two others on the scaffold give him a shove, and he travels a foot or so and stops.

They haul him back to the top, grease the slide more liberally, and give him a rougher shove. He flies off and bounces on the cement floor, the box frame of the camera flying apart like a prank substitute.

Freund huffs up the ladder for a look. His first assistant makes a quiet suggestion about raising the lip of the slide. Freund doesn't answer, and instead sends his fourth assistant across the room for the toolbox. The boy is lanky, hard of hearing, and open-mouthed. We watch him hunt for the toolbox. He gets low to bring his head closer to the search. He drifts. "You know, masturbation is a dreadful thing," Freund finally murmurs. The boy colors at our laughter.

I'M LATE for the last bit of casting, the role of the doorman's daughter.

Mayer is back at the sitting room outside my office, the folding chairs and old sprung ottoman already filled with candidates. They recognize him, thrilled to be in his presence. They regard me with puzzled interest, as if thinking, And I *should* know you, too. . . . All the women are taller than Mayer.

The first woman's features are too coarse, and her age too advanced. Despite that, there's something remarkable in her line readings—suggestive of venomous energy—and we tell her to keep in touch. She'll be of use, perhaps as one of the neighbors.

The fifth is perfect. A newcomer. When introduced, she thrusts out her hand with a shy abruptness. When we start to speak, she listens with flattering attention. Throughout she wears a look of piercing disappointment, as if she's already been rejected. We're both excited by her. Before our eyes, the role of the daughter takes shape. Thus the possibilities of leaving a character like a pencil sketch, to be filled in by the right person.

Despite her pessimism, upon leaving she kisses our cheeks

with perfect aplomb. I'm always attracted to poise in women. The untrained actress looking for work needs either unusual beauty or a thorough knowledge of her strengths. If she has the first, she usually possesses the second; if she has the second, she can make people believe she also has the first.

By that point, it's noon and everyone's yawning. Four hours have slipped away. The rest of the candidates are sent home. Lunch in my office, brought in, is shared with a German shepherd we've named Pal, who arrived out of nowhere and became a fixture around the studio once he realized the stagehands carried lunches to work. Just like that, the dog leads me to a memory of Hans, and an immovable sadness shoulders into the room. The anniversary of his death is a month away.

The dog whimpers and waits and, after what he considers a sufficient interval, eases my sandwich off its waxed paper and onto the floor. In two or three head-bobbing bites it's gone. I no longer have anyone who provides a sounding board for my nature.

I no longer have anyone with whom I can discuss the mysteries. I no longer have the certainty of being understood and answered. Now, whatever my current friendships, I have only this journal.

And yet for long stretches he disappears from my consciousness. I have made no headway as to the question of his death. For long stretches I seem to carry on regardless.

The dog gags and aspirates from eating too fast. Then the room is quiet. I call my car to take me home. I leave messages for Freund and Mayer to proceed in my absence.

The car is running poorly, and the chauffeur without ideas as to why. Why is there so much traffic at midday? He remarks on torrential rains in the south. Flooding in Bavaria. Hans, Hans, Hans. Only what's entirely lost demands to be endlessly named: the mania to call upon the lost thing until it returns.

A DAY and night devoted to mourning, and pointless calls around to our old acquaintances. Those I am able to reach are baffled by my questions. Sandri keeps his distance. With the new day, Frau Reger sits me up in bed and spoons potato soup into me. After taking away my tray, she returns to open the curtains and dump a pile of telephone messages onto the comforter.

MORE sleep.

A DISMAL few weeks of work. Mayer and Herlth ask discreet questions about my health. A month of shooting and already we're behind. Herlth and Röhrig keep wailing: more money! Fierce ongoing battles with Pommer, which fall to me to settle. My duties include, apparently, pedagogy and demagogy.

Yesterday a general meeting was called; I had to be driven back in for it. Pommer claimed he should stay out of it, and said I should speak for him.

Everyone was complaining as if the Apocalypse had arrived. The stipends were pitiful and unfair; the price of meat had gone up. What was I supposed to say? I sat there looking blank. The electricians delivered a declaration that they stood united behind the carpenters. And where did the carpenters stand? What did that mean? Had everyone lost their minds? Freund shushed me, and dealt with emissaries from both groups.

In terms of the inflation, the general situation is indeed catastrophic. That an undertaking like this is possible is a miracle. Emergency legislation and upbeat pieces on "What Every Citizen Can Do" fill the newspapers. A bitter winter is predicted. Or, rather, assured. A year ago it was even more dire. Then, the cashier at my pharmacy gave me change of two and a half million in five-thousand-mark notes, five packets as thick as two fists. How to get rid of them? A nice white shirt in a shopwindow, too expensive. A book? Ten million for a slim volume of Rilke. Instead, a café, the waiter willing to accept such small bills.

Germany was a house with the roof torn off, with the room-by-room disaster exposed for all to see. That night in a club, I watched a young American throw coins in his currency on the floor and call out that only naked women were allowed to pick them up. The eyes of the men in that room! But they did nothing. And two women, middle-aged, silently stripped off their clothes and got down on their knees.

I MUST wake earlier and get started sooner. In the morning I'm shrewdest, and most anxious, since anxiety is a form of shrewdness. Instead of six-a.m. starts, by five I'm up, but standing around gathering wool. Instead of tea I'll have tea and yoghurt; fruit later, to reward myself. I've taken to working in an old felt hat. Odd looks from the crew.

The *Tageblatt* Sunday supplement had a piece on the status of the production, entitled UFA'S 2 MILLION MARK GAMBLE. The sub-heading read *Unprecedented Battle of the Minds, While the Meter Clicks Away.* "Oh, obscenity the *Tageblatt*," Mayer said when he saw it. The phrase was immediately adopted as our rallying cry: Obscenity the *Tageblatt*.

WHILE THE camera agonies inch toward improvement, we work on simpler scenes with Jannings. For a while, everything is centered around him, which is one of the reasons the project delighted him so. Two interiors come off without incident: the doorman exhausted by his heavy load, accepting a drink and a rest; and the doorman waiting to see the manager. A metronome sets the rhythm for everyone's coming and going. Jannings performs with appropriate aplomb. It's occurred to everyone that this may be the role for which he was put on this earth.

Emboldened, we attempt the dream-sequence of him juggling the supersized trunks. A disaster. The cables are visible, and the trunks are clearly not being hefted by Jannings. He's no acrobat, and is continually nervous under all the spinning and colliding. He flinches and ducks, trying to hide his fear with a lot of operatic smiling. For a huge star, he's an interesting type: a man whose instincts come and go, like my own. I realize that I watch each take with my legs crossed, jogging my raised foot as if conducting the scene with my shoe. The crew has already figured out that when the shoe stops, I'm displeased.

COLLABORATION HAS always been a trial for me, since I want to carry everything about with me in silence, not wanting to share until the whole feels completed.

When I'd mentioned that to Hans, one giddy night in school when we'd been designing a parodic coat of arms for our room, his laughter quieted and he said, "That seems clear."

LANG HAS pointed out in a telegram wishing the project well that the tragedy we're filming could never occur, since no doorman would stoop to doing the job of a luggage porter or valet. "The old bitch," Jannings says when he hears.

AFTER LUNCH the script boy has mislaid the master notebook. Nothing can happen until he finds it. In its columns we register the date, scene number, characters, action, lighting, effects, camera stop number, and the amount of footage. Though he finds it again almost immediately, Freund dismisses him at the end of the day.

Ninety percent of my work consists of the secondary chores I perform in order to get to the other ten percent. Something always comes up. Everywhere an argument about who should run out to the café for sweets. The most relentless idiocies filter through. Today I received a bill for a goose that someone ordered in January.

EACH NIGHT, the same miseries, re-rehearsed in bed. Will the camera problems be worked out? Is it all too slow? Too ponderous? Trivial? Each morning, back in the car, exhausted by having been at odds with myself all night. Insufficient time to consider the best solutions to the problems at hand. Our work is an illustration of Zeno's paradox: since at each instant an arrow shot from a bow is stationary at some point in space, the succession of instants cannot constitute motion.

THE MOBILITY of the camera is even more crucial now that Mayer and I are firm on the revolutionary notion that *Der Letzte Mann* will have no titles. (!) We want the world of the story to proceed unimpeded, for the action to progress by visual means, the expressivity of the moving camera allowing us to dispense with the explanatory interruption. We want to make the audience a mass of common visionaries, obeying a law they did not know but recited in their dreams. For what we want—the camera swinging great distances through space—some means of stabilizing it is crucial. We need to hang it on a kind of sliding suspension bridge; we need it to follow the doorman through crowds, and up flights of stairs; we need it to drop from one balcony to another. So far, our unchained camera has been liberated only from its ability to provide a comprehensible image. The movements have been too complex and minute to allow the camera operator to adequately correct for stability. Our most recent solution was a metal dish-within-a-dish of ball bearings, which allowed the camera to swing freely. Too freely. The images we got looked like the chronicles of an earthquake.

Each day after principal shooting, we convene at Freund's makeshift laboratory to watch him wrestle with the problem. We toss out our own ideas, as well. So much metalworking is going on that the place looks like a foundry. Cellini and his assistants must have sweated and cursed before their ovens in the same way. A miserable summer on top of everything else. Freund had great holes torn into the walls for ventilation, to no avail.

An idea. Sketch it up. Work it out in steel and leather, cable and springs, whatever else you can find. Try it. Fix it, once it breaks. Try it again. After one disastrous block-and-cable affair, Freund lifted the whole apparatus over his head to destroy it before his assistants prevailed upon him to lower it safely to the ground. Day after day the problem torments him. He walks around bathed in the various oils he's using to produce a smooth rotation in the tilting mechanism. I'm reminded of Vischer's phrase about the perfidy of the object, which gloats upon our efforts to dominate it: that *Schadenfreude*, with its overtones of diabolical persistence.


WE KEEP telling ourselves that anything that can be imagined can be done, as Méliés has already demonstrated. When in despair, all we can do is act as if we believe, and faith may come afterwards. Meanwhile, off in the corner, Freund's fourth assistant sits, his mouth still ajar, before his assigned repair work, stuffing matchsticks into the stripped wooden threads of a tripod base.

ONE NIGHT I have dreams that I'm trying to master some sort of optical instrument by focusing on a flashing pinprick of light through an eyepiece. I wake to an electrical storm.

THE NEXT morning, no progress. Freund has been in the lab overnight. This is conveyed to us in low tones by his first assistant, whom we call the Kestrel because of his way of jerking his head toward the object of his attention.

There's also been a catastrophe with the courtyard set: the walls are bowing inward from the weight of the suspension cables. What will happen when we add the weight of both the camera and Freund? Röhrig's crew seems to have followed a set of earlier instructions with the kind of subconscious bitterness that develops in those accustomed to doing exactly what they're told. In the military this usually results in acts of heroism costing ninety-percent casualties.

Anticipating their mistake would have called for the kind of calm foresight of which I'm presently incapable. Lately I've been given more to panic than foresight. While what I can only glimpse slips away even as I try to prepare to film it.

ANOTHER WEEK lost. August! The year 1924 was supposed to bring bad luck: "Saturn complications." This we well believe.

LATE AFTERNOONS feature a stream of visiting strangers, as if on an incoming tide. Arranged by Pommer in hopes that the society pages might provide coverage. A baron, two bankers, a large

Pole whom no one can place, a conductor from a provincial orchestra, and a dancing countess—all visit as if stranded with no intention of leaving. They're all fascinated with Mayer, and frightened of Freund. The conductor is eager to discuss his theory of music-numerology with me because of certain structural patterns in my earlier films. Ufa executives also parade through to show their wives and mistresses how a big-time production is run. As if we needed any additional chaos. Still: "Keep smiling!" said the bird to the worm. . . . One of the visitors turns out to be the long-lost Lasker-Schüler, unsurprisingly in need of money. As far as my concerns go, money is no problem, but time is, and naturally she needs to explain in detail why she finds herself in such a state. She recounts a hectic series of recent affairs and claims that because of them, God has cured her with "the icy calm of not loving." Mayer, in the room for this announcement, sighs like a steam-hoist and leaves.

She's decked out in a fez and what looks like a chain-mail bustier. I ask about Paul. She answers that she's putting art aside for a while, to devote herself more fully to human matters.

Paul, it turns out, has developed tuberculosis. She was forced to sell what little they had to pay for his rest cures. Meanwhile he announced that he wants nothing to do with her; in the spring, once he's twenty-one, he wants to clear out and go round preaching with the Anabaptists or the vegetarians. She's unsure which.

Her problem, she says, has always been that her heart has played the leading role in her life. She reminds me that as a very little girl she alarmed her mother one night by seeing her pulsing heart hanging dark red on the doorpost of her playroom.

I keep her feet moving toward the door. I'll have my banker call her, I insist. He'll arrange for whatever's necessary. At the moment, though, an unavoidable bit of business—a crucial meeting, for which I'm already late—and she's out the door. My assistant appears, ready to show her out.

I make my goodbyes. Will she be around once all of this monstrousness has ended, in the late fall? She will, she says, and leaves it at that.

Back in my office, with the door shut between us, I hear her dismiss my assistant: she can find her own way out. Once his footsteps recede, she asks herself: "What am I going to do?" There's a pause. "What am I going to do?"

I open the door to call her back in, but she's gone.

ONE OF Freund's cameras on a trial run down the cable smashes itself to bits on the opposite wall below.

SANDRI DAY by day seems more disturbed. I find apple cores arranged to form a triangle under my pillow. Violent scribbles deface whatever's left lying about. Frau Reger terrified of him. She's caught him going through my drawers. To avoid him, she's taken to coming in late at night to clean. This all seems to be taking place in someone else's house. Usually I come back so late that she's gone and he's asleep, in various places.

The house seems uninhabited. My study looks like the last encampment of the nomad. At night I wander the halls, peering into other rooms.

THIS IDIOTIC compulsion to put up an act in front of the world, pretending everything is fine: that's what consumes so much of my energy.

In the early morning, my thoughts turn to other failures. Why is it only after people have gone that I'm able to take them into myself, the more deeply the farther away they are?

Filmmaking offers shelter for a failure to live. The essence it transfers to the medium is stolen from life. Without my note-books I'm ignorant, an absent curator for myself.

I tell myself, Write what comes, catch what you can as best you can. Once the notebook is filled, the spirit has calmed.


THE NEXT morning, in the carpenters' shop, I stand dazed beneath a yellow snowfall of sawdust. Neuralgia, sneezing fits, the beginnings of a bad cold. A fever coming. Röhrig suggests rum. "Röhrig always suggests rum," says Herlth. "Have you seen his nose?"


THE ELECTRICIANS and carpenters are unhappy with their coffee-and-sweets cart. The motto for this production, Jannings says, is "Somebody Should Do Something." I suggest it should be "We All Whine Together."

Mayer informs me at lunch that our decision to present the film without titles is considered by the crew to be the ultimate evidence of my haughtiness.


THE LATEST tilting mechanism swung too rapidly in its housing and crushed the fingers of the fourth assistant. In terms of the calendar, we're rapidly reaching the point at which the film will have to be reconceived. With increasing frequency I find notes from Pommer on my desk about the cost of our experiments. In my one note back, I quoted Goethe: *Nothing injures the treasury more than the endeavor to save in essential matters.*


WE'RE SATISFIED, at least, with the sling/basket arrangement in which Freund will sit. It hangs from its suspension bridge like a reinforced swing for an unbelievably heavy child. Freund sits with both feet splayed in the direction the apparatus will travel.

FINALLY, ONE day he sends down word of an announcement. We all gather round, down to the lowest stagehand. Pal worms his way forward, sniffing. The shops are quiet. Freund and the Kestrel work within a circle of spectators. Some of the female extras, chorus girls, push forward from the back, tittering and shoving. Pommer murmurs, "A little more virginity, ladies." Then all is quiet.

In a low voice as he works, Freund explains a new version of a gyroscope that's electronically controlled. The mechanism operates off a carpenter's level with triggers on both ends: as the bubble moves off center, electrical impulses send more or less power, as needed, to the small balancing motors.

A test: we all hold our breath. The housing still jiggles. Wait— one trigger not working. An adjustment. Freund climbs into his basket, and the mechanism is lowered onto his lap. Together they're hoisted to the top of the suspension bridge, everyone taking a turn on the ropes.

The stagehands wait for his signal.

Down he swings, his eye to the eyepiece.

Herlth, Röhrig, Mayer, Pommer, myself—everyone surges forward, waiting. At the end of the cable, the basket sways back and forth, tipping slightly. Freund's face is still screwed to the eyepiece.

"Here it is," he says quietly.

The Kestrel laughs, his laugh on the order of a seizure. It's the only sound anyone makes before a roar goes up from everyone.

FREUND'S VERDICT has to be confirmed by the rushes. It is, that night.

After that, our giddiness sends him and his camera everywhere: up a swaying fireman's ladder. Down an open lift. Around on a bicycle. Across great expanses on a rubber-wheeled trolley. There's so much cheering and laughter on the set that visitors believe us to be drunk.

And finally we propose as another vehicle Freund's stomach, with the batteries on his back as a counterweight. "It's too heavy," he protests. "I'll hurt my back." Nonsense, we tell him. We strap it on and he sets about the lot, weaving and tripping. He follows Jannings like a shadow, bending, twisting, and leaning. Within a quarter of an hour, he's hurt his back.

TIME AT the studio increases. Some nights I go home at four and return at six. We work as long as our energy holds. Every midnight, Mayer and I repair to the projection room to run the day's footage and marvel at what we've done. Two projectionists divide the work between them. There we sit, hour after hour, studying the images. How best to use them and improve their effect? Late into the night, we muse aloud: If we took the last of number 3 and the first of number 6 . . . Hours spent organizing these new miracles of movement. And then I'm driven home, the car floating past darkened houses where everyone is asleep. I close my eyes in my bedroom, still uncertain whether the last temporary decision was the right one.

Throughout all of this I come to understand that the horrible days of exhaustion and powerlessness may be part of my work method.

I lie in bed, unable to sleep: happy, happy, happy. Sandri agitated by my new emotional state.

What I see in advance is the beauty of the entire film coming together.

The rainstorm of the opening sequence. Surfaces streaming with rain and light as the camera plays along them.

The view through the lift-window as it descends, and the camera's ride through the lobby.

The noise of the horn reaching the doorman's ears: the sound moving visually from the horn's mouth to Jannings, three stories above.

His Exposure. The Maliciousness of the Hens—of the Beehive. The Glee of the Secret Revealed. The Truth spread like a contagion. The camera swinging from balcony to balcony, from mouth to ear. Humiliation. Ruin. The superimposition of overlapping mouths.

And the newest footage: Jannings in the lavatory's darkness, caught by the night watchman's torch. The camera's kindness, as it too moves to stroke the crown of his head.


TERROR AT home. Sandri inexplicably terrified and enraged at the sight of Mayer.

I try not to shout. Sandri seems to fear for his life. He upends furniture to keep me back. He barricades himself into Frau Reger's room, and resists efforts to push open the door.

Mortified, I apologize to Mayer and arrange to have us driven back to the studio. Mayer is silent all the way back. I'm stomach-sick with fear.

At the studio, all is quiet. Mayer heads off to his workspace.

In my office, the telephone's ringing off the hook. When I answer, it's the police. Sandri has run amok. He's bludgeoned Frau Reger and pitched her body into the street. The police have the house cordoned off and surrounded.


THE HOUSE is stormed. They find him in my bedroom. He fractures one policeman's skull before he's shot to death.


DER LETZTE MANN premieres at the Ufa-Palast am Zoo, which boasts 2,165 seats and, since its opening in 1919 with Lubitsch's

*Passion,* has been the uncontested flagship of Ufa's theaters. Ventilation is supplied by a miniature electric zeppelin three feet long which drifts through the house during intermissions and sprays eau de cologne about with an atomizer. There are standing ovations even before the final curtain. Jannings pulls me up out of the audience. The adulation washes over us in waves.

THERE'S HARDLY time, that week, for Frau Reger's funeral. Sandri is buried in a field for transients. Late at night, when the schedule permits, my chauffeur drives me there. On each visit, I'm reminded of a moment from the premiere: the solitary figure of Jannings, which became Sandri, which became Hans, and then, finally, only a dumb image, which quivered for a moment on the screen and then disappeared.

# TABU

****14/15 JUNE 1929 (Midnight). No sleep. All afternoon, the trace odor of land, unmistakable after eight weeks of open sea. Toward sunset we began to notice the scent of flowers. *Cassi,* David informed us: a low, bushlike plant that carpets the Marquesas.


FRIEDRICH WILHELM MURNAU, filmmaker in the Republic of Germany from 1919 to 1925, and in the United States of America from 1926 to 1929, was spending May and June of 1929 in a ketch halfway between Mexico and New Zealand. For three straight nights he had slept only one or two hours. He was writing on deck. The cockpit bench was rigged like a divan with throw-pillows. Pal was curled at his feet. The dog's tongue lolled about. The sea air made the poor animal endlessly thirsty.

The moon went all the way down. Before he lit the lamp, he could see his hand in the starlight.

They had traveled southwest by west from Mazatlán to Nukahiva, in the Marquesas. It was one of the few long traverses in the Pacific where the direct course was also the fastest.

Sometime the next day he would get his first view of the South Seas. Sitting there on the deck, every so often he would write: *The South Seas!* He had constructed a little column of such exclamations. From there to Papeete, some 400 miles, would be about four days.

Anxiety piled up behind his excitement the way a wake surge overtook smaller waves. All those lives transformed to suit his purposes: seventeen intelligent men who'd never been far from pavement were about to be marooned across those isolated islands. Their average age was twenty-three.

He fretted constantly that this project, in ways none of the group could fully understand, was bigger than any studio-made film. With a studio, the world was built to suit the filmmaker. But here! Eighteen thousand dollars had already been forwarded not for sets and mysterious union "overheads," but to natives for food, transport, shelter, carpenters, carriers, divers, fishermen, and brush-clearers. This was the first time he'd seen *brush-clearing* listed as an expense.

And to all that he had to add the for-him-unprecedented difficulties of collaboration. One of the world's great geniuses of romantic illusion, at least if his American press clippings were to be believed, had thrown in with the pre-eminent cinematic practitioner of the real. NOSFERATU MEETS NANOOK, *Variety* had teased. In this case, both maestros were wary. Murnau had never worked with a partner, however collaborative his early experience in Germany had been; and Robert Flaherty's only partner had been his wife. Occasionally he'd take a suggestion from his long-suffering cameraman.

They had agreed on the concept of an epic shot in spectacular natural locations, which was, after all, the Grail of nearly every national cinema. Flaherty's *Nanook of the North,* they further agreed, was the closest anyone had come to date. So they wanted to transport their audience, and involve it in an exotic and endangered way of life. But after that?

After That, they'd decided to put off until their arrival in Tahiti.

Flaherty's younger brother, David, was traveling with Murnau. Eight weeks out of Mazatlán, they were reveling in the good weather after a week of uninterrupted rain. That week they had all been insomniacs. Their hands had turned white and wrinkled;

their feet, when they undressed, looked like dead sea creatures. Only the caviar, preserved on ice, had raised their spirits. Each evening they'd huddled around warm tea and cold caviar, giving thanks for the French consulate in Mazatlán.

MURNAU AND Flaherty were both unhappy refugees from Fox. Flaherty's film on Mexican Indians had collapsed when Fox himself had taken it over. Murnau's *Four Devils* and *Our Daily Bread* had the same sorry history. David had joked that they should've pooled their catastrophes and cut the release prints together to make *Indian Bread*.

For three straight weeks, Murnau had watched despondently while the undercooked meat was pulled from the bones of his picture. He met with Fox and his Brain Trust in their private screening room, where they indulged in a ritual of mutilation and humiliation. He was unable to eat and suffered spells of dizziness. Faces he'd never seen before offered advice and made insulting remarks about his work. He held his tongue. What was wrong with it? Everything was wrong. He was doing the same old thing again; the film was too long; the peasants weren't American; the story had no "zing." The whole thing was too *ponderous*, Fox himself said; it was as though everyone was walking around in heavy boots.

Murnau's responses were not appreciated. He and Fox each took a turn with some invective. Then Fox suggested that his overworked artiste take a break and let the boys fiddle with a few things. Murnau remarked that he'd seen enough of the boys' fiddling. He was banned from the screening room.

Once more the gagmen had been set to work. Fox sent conciliatory memos. Murnau terminated his contract. The film was taken over by an honest man with no imagination and reissued under a different title. When Murnau wrote him with seven pages of modifications he thought might save the picture, he never received an answer.

The day it had been taken out of his hands, he sought refuge by himself in a Mexican restaurant. The one other patron in the place—seeming to have a notion that the tall, freckled, miserable man occupying the opposite booth was distraught—had a pink-colored drink with a miniature paper hat sent over. The teetotaling Murnau removed the hat and lifted the drink every so often, in order to indicate his appreciation without sipping.

Since the collapse of the film, his kidneys had resumed causing him great distress and any time in the sun made him feel faint.

Then Berthold Viertel had come in with a familiar-looking blond boy in tow, whom he introduced. David had Hans's mouth and hair, as well as a similar way of standing, like an adolescent wishing to seem barrel-chested. They chatted about Murnau's work, which caused Murnau to perk up a little.

He perked up a little more when he realized that David's brother was *that* Flaherty. The patron who'd sent over the drink seemed discouraged, as though he'd missed his opportunity.

Murnau had long admired Flaherty's work. He asked an hour's worth of questions, all of which David answered straightforwardly. Flaherty was still working on the Mexican film. For the first time, David was assisting.

After leaving the restaurant, they walked to a deserted triangle of park and settled on a bench beneath a eucalyptus tree. The smell seemed to revive the discussion. Viertel sat quietly alongside the two new friends, content to listen. Sap on the seat slats ruined Murnau's trousers.

Flaherty turned out to be four years older than Murnau. Did the brothers have any new plans, for after the Mexican project? They did: David had been preparing to go away that very week to Tahiti, to assess the possibilities of filming a feature there.

Murnau at that moment felt as if he'd become aware of great

gears above them swinging together, the teeth sliding inexorably into place. Once he recovered, he described in a low voice how he'd dreamed of doing the same thing. This did not seem to impress his audience. He added that he'd read about the South Seas since discovering Stevenson as a boy. They smiled. His dizziness had returned. He'd had to call for his car.

David left for Tahiti two days later, and Murnau hadn't seen him again for three months. During that interval, he worked listlessly on new projects. Fox sent over scripts that had been defaced and rejected by other contract directors.

The day after David returned, they ate alone in Murnau's newest place in the Hollywood hills. The domestic staff had been instructed to prepare the meal and leave. The two men served themselves from a banquette. Pal sat in his wingbacked chair and kept an eye on both of them.

The dining table had a view of Los Angeles. They reviewed the charts and drawings David had brought back. They laughed about his inability to eat for all of Murnau's questions. For stretches Murnau just stared at the navigational map of the Tuamotus. He reminded himself of the Nosferatu peering over Hutter's papers while his guest apprehensively dined.

He told David about the yacht he'd bought, which he'd renamed the *Bali*. Other than that, he said, he'd spent the last few months making the round of kidney specialists. Hollywood, he concluded, was wearing him out. He was getting too old for this, now nearly forty-one, and had no heart left for battling the studio.

Commiserating, David looked as if he recognized forty-one to be Methuselan.

That look prompted Murnau to announce that he was going to the South Seas. There was a pause. He asked if David would accompany him.

David, dumbfounded, answered that he was obliged to rejoin his brother in Mexico. Murnau had swung into action as his old

persuasive self. That Flaherty's film was at the point of being suspended was an open secret around the Fox lot; even Murnau had
been privy to that news. So why shouldn't they all join forces,
then, and make a film after their own hearts, in Tahiti?

David had had certain hesitations. Murnau asked: Shouldn't
brothers seize every opportunity to work together? He stayed at
it, selling his enthusiasm far into the night. He himself, of course,
had neglected his connections with his own brothers for years.

The next day, they set off in his new red Packard to convince
Flaherty, whose funding was stalled in Tucson. The doctors had
been unanimous that the trip would be disastrous for Murnau's
kidneys. They proved correct. The pain became difficult before
they'd left the city limits, and they had to make frequent stops.
Murnau spent the night of their arrival in a clinic. In between,
there'd been three days of the sort of good talk he hadn't had in
years, and excited planning. He told David about Hans: about his
poetry, the intensity of their relationship, their estrangement, and
Hans's death in the war before that estrangement could be
addressed. David knew some of the poetry in translation, from an
old compendium of verses from the war dead entitled *The Flower
of German Youth*.

Flaherty had seized upon their idea. He visited Murnau that
first night in the clinic and described with precision his idea of the
most memorable images from *Nosferatu* and *Faust,* which he'd just
seen. He'd particularly admired the vampire's ship gliding into
Bremen harbor, and the Devil's pestilential cloak spreading over
Faust's little medieval hamlet.

From his bed of pain, Murnau reciprocated by describing how
exalted he'd been upon seeing *Nanook*.

Flaherty was much impressed that Murnau had driven all that
way in such trying circumstances to work with him. In seven days
they'd worked up a proposal for a joint project and negotiated and
signed a contract with a new company, Colorart, that had

approached Flaherty. The new contract, in terms of freedom, was a dream; it stipulated no company presence on location, and the whole picture would be made on location! By the 18th of April, a budget of one hundred and fifty thousand dollars had been approved. Murnau and David would sail from San Pedro at the end of the month. Flaherty would leave a month later by steamship with the crew and supplies.

SPIESS WAS still out there, somewhere near where they were going. Murnau had proof. Recently he'd been getting a series of "gifts" through the mails: badly wrapped seashells, carved bits of bone (one labeled "Sea-Monster!"), and lumpen charms and amulets. They'd been sent to Murnau's original Los Angeles address. The last package featured a rough squatting figure with a head split in two, on the back of which was carved *H.E.-D:* Hans's initials. It had been wrapped in a handbill advertising a showing of *Dernier des Hommes: Der Letzte Mann,* on which someone had scribbled in German *How's this for worldwide success—your name now known in Bali. Heading east. Hecate.* Murnau had been pained by the reference to their schoolboy recitations: Hans as Medea, himself as Jason.

In eight years he had made no progress on the question of Hans's suicide. He fought the notion that no progress was possible. Lasker-Schüler had passed along a few letters Hans had written to her, and then she had refused any further help. In the letters, Hans mentioned neither suicide nor Murnau. Other old friends and acquaintances were less helpful still. Hans's commanding officer had been killed in the Spartacists' uprising after the war. Only Spiess remained.

While Murnau had been waiting for David to return from Tahiti, a boy he'd hired to monitor Pacific shipping transactions had sent word that an "E. J. Spies" had been one of three partners at Papeari, east of Samoa, who'd been hoping to barter copra for a thirty-foot yawl. The other two partners had been listed as "Robert Dean Frisbie, writer" and "Ropati, speculator."

Spiess was his last hope of proving Lasker-Schüler wrong. It had come down to that. In one of the letters, Hans had mentioned writing Spiess. This was the last lead Murnau had. In any event, securing the proper cast and locations would mean travel among the islands. His plan was to comb the groups east to west for Europeans fitting Spiess's description, and then to keep an ear out once shooting began.

THE *BALI* was long and slim, sixty-five feet by sixteen feet, drawing eight and half feet of water. She belonged to the Gloucester Fisherman class, with two sails and a fifty-horsepower engine. Below, beside the galley and the crew's quarters, there was a dining room, a stateroom, a lavatory, and a pantry. She flew both the American and the German flags. On her stern Murnau had painted a blood-red heart.

THE MAINSAIL luffed and billowed above him in the darkness. The helmsman, Bill Bambridge, had one leg encased in plaster and leaned on his crutch like Long John Silver. He hadn't spoken in hours.

WHEN PAL needed to defecate, he climbed up on the back deck and did his business off the taffrail in calm seas. In rough seas he sat around whining. At such times, David murmured his general disbelief at the dog's presence.

For Murnau the whole trip had been a blessed relief from physical infirmities. He'd rigged a collapsible silken canopy for the cockpit, and for long stretches he would close his eyes and relax his body and listen to the hissing rush of water along the hull. In his journal he copied a verse from the American Emerson: *And the lone seaman all the night / Sails astonished among stars.* When he dozed, he dreamt of their departure from San Pedro, and the California mud on the anchor flukes as it came up. When he woke, there always seemed to be an extra stillness in the air. The only sound was the musical liquid noise of their wake. In the east over the stern, the lower quadrant was the orange of embers, the binnacle lamp already dull against the coming brightness of the day. There were stirrings below. David climbed up the companionway and replaced Bambridge at the helm with a pre-dawn regard for silence. Pal gave himself a good shake and went below for water.

Murnau stood and worked out the kinks. He was stiff and chilly. He stretched. He checked the stars to assure himself that he'd truly arrived at this place so far from what he knew, then headed forward. The breeze smelled of morning. He settled on the foredeck between the windlass and an open hatch, his knees pulled to his chin. Eddy, their Japanese cook, clanked around below making coffee. There was a clinking in Pal's dish.

That was how he was sitting, smelling coffee and flowers and the sea, when he sighted landfall: Taio-haie, on Nukahiva.


THE CLOSER they got, the brighter the colors became. They needed new eyes for this. They were all on deck, their gaze on the scarped and shattered peaks that protected the inner loop of the bay. Around the bay, the white reefs were as delicate as lace.

Pal was all the way out on the bowsprit. A white thread of a waterfall cascaded thousands of feet down the steepest of the cliffs to break into mist below. David informed them that it was Typee Falls, from the Typee valley.

Around the black point of the escarpment, the panorama of

the bay opened out. A file of houses lined the white sand behind coconut palms and thickets with crimson flowers. Murnau could make out cassi, frangipani, and the evergreen smell of oleander.

David pointed out that he was weeping.

Bambridge said, "He's been weeping for the last fifteen minutes."

THEY BEAT in three tacks into the bay through the first smooth water they'd seen since San Pedro, six fathoms deep. They looked overboard to the bottom the way they might look down from a fourth-story window on a sunny day.

A whaleboat piloted by a native guided them to their anchorage. A white-haired Frenchman in a military jacket and sailcloth pants announced himself as Harbormaster and Chief of Police, and brought them ashore.

MURNAU'S INITIAL contact with the native population was with a few dockworkers. He was surprised at their sullenness. They distrusted Pal and stared without smiling as they went about their work. Most of the women were missing teeth. A hundred years before, the Frenchman informed him, the Marquesas had had a population of one hundred and forty thousand; now, thanks to the white man, a thousand were left.

THEIR TEMPORARY quarters were overrun with ants. They napped instead on the beach, on shaded benches and tables. The unshaded sunlight was stunning. The Harbormaster drowsed where he sat, opposite Murnau, his hand still on his glass of lemonade. Pal crouched beneath a table with ears down and chin low. Enormous yellow flowers called burao fell heavily, as if from the heat, onto the sand; the sound was like a dropped cap.

Still, Murnau was unable to sleep. He was beginning to understand how much time, patience, and work would be required to capture any part of the shattered and fugitive splendor of the islands. The land was not the issue. What he'd have to search for everywhere were men with the pride, the beauty, and the independence he'd imagined in their ancestors.

No one on Nukahiva remembered Spiess. The Harbormaster remembered someone named Thun or Thule, whom he was sure had been a Dane.

A week later they successfully negotiated the Passe de Fakarava, an emerald channel flanked by shoals. It was the last step involved in threading the treacherous Paumotos, listed on the charts as the Low or Dangerous Archipelagoes.

Bambridge had worked the charts and Murnau the helm. At some points the coral shelves had glided by only meters from their hull. The shoals churned white water into the air. A fine mist soaked everything. Rainbows bisected their masts.

Once back in open water, they congratulated themselves on their seamanship. Eddy took the wheel. Flying fish appeared off their windward side, following the ship.

They took a ponyback trip over three-thousand-foot mountain passes into the valley of Typee to view the spot where Melville had been held prisoner. Pal was trounced by a wild pig. They made a pilgrimage to Gauguin's grave at Atuona. On the gravestone someone had scrawled the painter's words: *All that your civilization gives rise to produces only disease.*

They were told that the sort of natives they were looking for might be found in Ua-Pou, close by to the south, since it was rocky and infertile and off the usual shipping routes. Sailing south-west to Takapoto, they witnessed the sobering industrial ugliness of the copra trade. They passed waterfront hovels of corrugated iron. On one of the nearby atolls, they had lunch and a paddle around the lagoon with Matisse the painter. He gave Murnau a tour of his makeshift studio. He was amused at Pal's South Seas adventure: this German dog, on a tour of the tropics. Murnau talked with him about the light and colors. David photographed them in a dugout with Pal and a native boy. Matisse wore a pith helmet for the photo, like Dr. Livingstone.

Matisse was skeptical about their plans, though he thought the islands were full of legends well suited to a photoplay. He mentioned the pearl-fishers who dived despite the peril of sharks; a giant crayfish that was said to seize its victims in its claws and hold them to drown in a nearby lagoon; the wide-eyed conger that lived in the coral caves.

He had run across no one like Spiess. But he'd just arrived himself, after all.

He complained at length about the Chinese merchants.

He gave Murnau a new hat with sombrero-like dimensions.

He was the last stop before Tahiti.

****30 JUNE.    11 p.m. Papeete, bathed in a sea of light, rising up out of the black water and a thousand beams.

****1 JULY.    The first full day in Tahiti, and things could not be worse. The production is at a standstill. Flaherty met us at the quay and welcomed us to Tahiti. He asked after his brother's asthma and announced that no money had been forwarded to meet them. The entire company has apparently lived on credit for the last two months.

This we learned at or about midnight. Even Pal was exhausted. We were drawn up along the stern of someone's monstrously large motor-yacht, the *Dissolution*. All its cabins were lit, and its occupants in the midst of a frenzied celebration of some sort. While we toiled to secure the *Bali* for the night in a moderate swell, Flaherty tried his best to provide details of the disaster over the noise from the yacht. Champagne glasses from its decks plunked into the water around us.

The contract with Colorart was by all indications meaningless. Flaherty had sent seven cables before an answering cable, unsigned, had confirmed the bankruptcy. I imagined some melancholy functionary, the last one at his desk, taking pity on him.

After a sleepless night, I spent my first morning in Tahiti in the telegraph office. I might as well be in Mazatlán. Cables to lawyers, cables to banks, cables to Viertel and Garbo imploring them to run various errands. The crisis was averted only when I finalized the arrangements to finance the film myself, from the remainder of my savings.

Flaherty was informed. His gratitude seems insufficient.

The next item of business is to pay off the crew, and the other debts already outstanding. Strained meetings with Flaherty, who is penniless. He acts as if he's the Artist and I'm the Producer. I know the tone. David attends looking exhausted and hungover.

My savings will not extend to cover the company's salaries. Even Flaherty's friends back in America are, of course, without a cent.

Nearly everyone has to be let go, including the unit manager and the laboratory man. Even Bambridge and Eddy the cook. Money is set aside to cover their passage home, with the wan promise of additional compensation later. Only Floyd Crosby, the principal cameraman, will stay and draw pay. The rest of the crew will have to be recruited locally.

Flaherty says he can run the laboratory himself, and train

native assistants. Crosby will do the trickier sailing, with native help. David will take over as unit manager, and assistant to all of us.

****A DESOLATE afternoon spent trying to nap in Papeete's Grand Hotel, the Hotel Montparnasse. Noisome and cacophonous even at midday. The toilet in the hall features a courteous little notice in French: "Will uncertain gentlemen please avoid the floor?" Judging from the floor, the adjective refers to breeding rather than aim.

We are forced, for the time being, into the Montparnasse. Even with a breeze, the *Bali*'s cabins are too hot at midday. I share my room with an oversized brown-and-yellow spider, both of us enervated by the heat.

AT TWILIGHT they took advantage of the cooler air for a meeting aboard the ship. Fourteen tons of equipment unloaded from the freighter were heaped under waxed tarpaulins and a makeshift shelter near the docks. That included the lighting generator, the spare cameras, the toolboxes, two projectors, the endless crated cannisters of raw film, and all the apparatus for the developing laboratory.

Had Flaherty looked into the possibilities for the safer storage of such materiel? He had not. What were the possibilities, Murnau wanted to know. Flaherty outlined a few. The best option seemed to be an unused portion of a copra trader's metal-roofed warehouse. Flaherty promised to approach the man the next morning.

After the meeting, Murnau went off by himself for a cheap meal and a cheerless walk. Papeete looked like a dismal metropole of the South Seas. Automobiles and omnibuses roared along the shore. The streets were lit by electric lights. Cinemas and dance halls and cabarets and Chinese restaurants blared their music out into the moonlight.

What have I done? he asked himself.

Later, to cheer him up, Flaherty led him to the other end of town, where a dilapidated movie house with a sheet of corrugated metal for a door advertised on its display board a film called *Sœur Angelique,* "Directed by F. Murnau." Flaherty found the announcement funny. What did it mean? There was no way to know. The movie house, Flaherty said, had apparently been closed for some time.

OVER THE next few days, Murnau's spirits began to recover. In the mornings he took breakfast—limes with sugar, a mango, a roll, and a pot of black coffee—on the Montparnasse's veranda, facing the peaks of Moorea. By seven o'clock they were flooded with morning light.

The crags and slopes of the volcanic islands of Oceania seemed to him so steep and wicked-looking that the coastlines, with their pale lagoons, looked gentle by contrast. There was always a scrap of mist around the peaks, and that unsettling below-the-horizon boom of surf on the invisible reefs. The population seemed to live entirely on the fringes of inaccessible slopes, so the villages appeared small and crowded.

Their materiel was safe in the copra trader's warehouse. The cost was a dollar a week, payment deferred. The trader had accepted two bottles of whisky as down payment.

Crosby had been spending his days in the warehouse with the film stock, trying to account for ten thousand feet of negative that probably had never been loaded aboard in San Pedro.

There had been some good news. After the break with Colorart, Murnau and Flaherty had needed to evolve a new story to free them of legal worries, and after three days of collaboration, had settled on the idea of the *tabu* as the film's centerpiece. The basic premise had come from Flaherty's experiences in Samoa. Murnau was excited by the possibilities: an impossible love, stalked by the same implacable transgression that enabled it.

After work in the afternoons they would cruise out into Papeete's crowded harbor. Beneath the green volcanoes, the water was a numinous blue, hardly sea-colored at all, with stunning depths and shallow coral shelves knobbed and ribbed like bones, rippling with fish. The water like candy-colored liqueurs in glass bottles in bars, lit from below. And at the end of the day, the sun now behind them, Moorea's mountains loomed dark and spiky, backlit. Local myths claimed them to be the dorsal fins of giant fish. To Murnau they looked more sinister than that, and more alluring. He imagined himself up there, spread across those waterless peaks.

EARLY IN the morning when the town was just stirring, he continued to pursue his discreet inquiries concerning Spiess. He ran into Flaherty on one expedition, and afterward imagined that Flaherty regarded him with suspicion.

TO SAVE money, they moved eleven kilometers out of town, to the old Governor's Residence. The Residency supposedly had all the comforts of a club. In this case, that included a bulletin board, a modest liquor cabinet, a map of the world on Mercator's projection, and a flyspecked portrait of Clemenceau over the bar. Still, it was out of Papeete, and it did feature the most spectacular view available on any veranda in the tropics.

Their fellow guests, French officials and Scottish merchant clerks, spent their time gossiping about the four moviemakers whose plans had come to such obvious grief.

The house was commodious. All day long, wide, louvered doors stood open and allowed the trades to blow over the bare floors. On weekdays the garden was filled with convicts, who set aside spade or barrow and touched their hats like old family servants whenever guests would pass. On weekends the convicts were gone. Dogs of all sizes took their place, sprawling wherever there was shade as if in the aftermath of battle. Pal kept his distance.

BEHIND THE Residency, a ruined wall overhung with acacia encompassed the European cemetery. Flaherty gave Murnau and David a tour. There were a few Germans here and there. One slab chipped in half read *Veidt*. Flaherty made a joke about *The Cabinet of Dr. Caligari,* and wondered if such projects always attracted homosexuals. Murnau let the comment go for a moment, then announced flatly that Veidt was a friend.

****8 JULY. Disagreements with Flaherty starting to become more serious. Flaherty claims that I Europeanize the Polynesians. I claim he cannot purge *Nanook* from his head. I try to make him see that the South Seas make unnecessary the epic virtues on which he seeks to build his stories. This is not the Arctic. The sea is not a relentless enemy. The land here is so rich that "farming" is beside the point. Here, love is the source of conflict. For me, the collapse of the old ways is part of the story; for him, it's the whole story.

David stays out of the debate, perching unhappily on his nearby camp stool while we fight. Sometimes he seems to be quietly stupefied. He and his brother have the same wide foreheads and bankers' frowns. At times it's as if Hans has returned, only to disapprove of me.

Crosby also sits in, hatless in the sun. He brings to the table a general impression of powerlessness and gloomy fatalism. He has always just washed his hair, which is thinning and blond.

After three days of argument, Flaherty banged the tabletop and announced that he wanted to stop talking about love. He wasn't interested in my private fantasies. He was interested in these islands. In the silence that followed, Crosby lowered his head to the table and moaned, "It was at that point that their difficulties really began."

I lay in bed afterwards, sleepless as usual, thinking, I left bitter dispute behind in Los Angeles so that I'd find it here, in the most beautiful place on earth?

****9 JULY.   Rain.

****10 JULY.   More rain. Impasse with Flaherty. He and David gone on a three-day expedition into the interior. Yrs truly not invited. Squirreled myself away on the *Bali* with my South Seas volumes: Stevenson, Loti, Nordhoff and Hall. Trying to cheer myself with the thought that it's also possible, despite my pessimism, that inspiration will find *me*— I notice I've begun to find myself quoting Stevenson's language.

****11 JULY.   Miracles———!
Where to begin? Yesterday while the rain drummed down, I heard a thumping on deck. I came up the companionway and there on the other side of the weather sheet stood a boy, streaming water. He'd swum out to see me. He felt no fear. He spoke a little French.

He refused tea but accepted hot water with lemon and sugar. He seemed to relish it. I gave him one of my sweaters. He had perfect teeth and glittering eyes. A coconut palm was tattooed along the length of his spine. The palm's crown flowered across his shoulders.

His fingers were small and graceful. He was a foot shorter than me and gave his age as seventeen. He was from Fatuhiva, an orphan.

I had only one lamp lit and the wind picked up. He noticed the Nordhoff and Hall open to an illustration of native customs and he rose, keeping his head low in the cramped space, and danced the *taprita* in slow silence. It was a dance in which the body moved more than the feet, the hips rolling sideways and forwards with perfect freedom. He took off my sweater, rolled it up, and pressed it between his legs with both palms. I was speechless.

****CONSCIOUS OF the need to step carefully. I want to conjure up and imprint the memory. I want for myself, for the future, a promptbook.

****I SAID, in English, "You are very beautiful." He looked at me the way he might watch a wave roll in. He joined me on the settee berth. He touched his fingers to my ear to register how much I was trembling. He turned my face to his. He raised his lips close, so that I could feel his warmth.

He was still. The rain had stopped. The fittings were dripping and the rudder creaked. He had the most grace of anyone I had ever seen. I closed my eyes and gave myself over to him. He cradled my face with his hands. He lifted me with surprising ease.

****WRITING THIS at 3 a.m. Moonless sky outside the hatch.
Tahiti is the New Cythera, the abode of Venus. When Venus

rose from the sea, she stepped ashore (according to Hesiod) at Cythera. De Bougainville was right: this is the world before the Fall. All the creatures associated with Venus are found here: the dolphin, the tortoise, and the gentlest birds. The frigate birds are so tame they have red streamers trailing from their legs to keep them safe from hunters.

****2 p.m. The curtains drawn and pinned. Rocking in and out of sleep as if in a fever. The boy calls himself Mehao. He's indicated he will leave at nightfall. He dozes on the floor with one foot in the linen locker. His gentleness and insatiability are revelatory. He holds my sex in his hand as if born to do so. When it slips from his grasp, I make sure it finds its way back to him.

I notice that for these notes I've reverted to German, as if for greater security.

****AMAZED AT what I've written down. For some sort of delectation later.

****12 JULY. 6 a.m. Nightmares about Hans. Horrible stomach upheavals. Mehao gone.

In the one I remember best, Hans again discovered my betrayal, and again I saw his face. Then the scene changed to a vegetable garden in bright sun.

Some straightening-up of the cabin. The smell of the last twenty-four hours is overpowering. I breathe it in like a tuberculosis patient. I can't bring myself to rig the windsail to air it out.

Overwhelmed by that familiar sense of ugliness and corruption. The portrait of Hans in his uniform is in the sea chest in the overhead locker, wrapped in oilskin.

Weeping.

****9 a.m.  A foray at regaining control. The attempt begins
with a good washing, on a rope hanging from the stern. Miniature
fish nibble at my toes. Even at the apex of my self-disgust, some
part of me begins musing about Mehao's whereabouts.

Bora-Bora    25 July 1929

*Mother!*

*I've no excuse for being such a bad correspondent, despite the
chaos and excitement of the last few weeks. Mea maxima etc.*

*We've arrived. All in all, with the good luck and the bad,
with the most wonderful days and the stormy, squally days,
we've had a glorious trip which none of us will ever forget. It's
been the fulfillment of a happy dream, surpassing all
expectations.*

*The trans-Pacific sail was a triumph. If you could have seen
your Wilhelm as sea-captain! All our ports of call in the South
seas were French possessions, and in none of these places had
the German flag been flown since the war. We'd been warned
that the natives might act strangely, as the war was still alive
with them. But instead, wherever we appeared we were received
with hospitality of a sort that only one who's been to Polynesia
can realize.*

*While the idea was to cruise as far west as possible, until
west met east, we're also, of course, hard at work on the picture.
It'll be called*

TABU
A Story of the South Seas

*and is based on the paradise-like conditions of some of the
islands here. To keep the spirit of the thing, we're staying away
from white actors and professionals. All those chosen, whether
half-caste or native, have never been in front of a camera before.*

*You know and understand that for a dramatic story this will be quite an experiment—but I'll enjoy doing it, and I hope to catch some of the true unspoiled Polynesian spirit, which, if we succeed, ought to be well worth the harder work.*

*We've gathered our cast from some of the remotest corners of these island groups, after testing hundreds of people. We believe now that we have the very best, and we start shooting soon. I'm sending some photographs of our main characters. We think that while they have all the qualities of the pure native appearance, they'll still appeal to a white audience. Personally, I think that with their charm and grace, they'd be a sensation if they entered European or American studios.*

*I'm also sending along some pictures of the trip. On the back of each I've given a short indication of what it is and where it was taken. You might want to contact Kurt Korff at Ullstein's; if he wants to publish any in Illustrierte Zeitung or Querschnitt, I expect you to drive a hard bargain! All pictures must carry the note "Murnau-Flaherty Production," marked on the back of the print. One, you will notice, features the painter Matisse. . . . If you sell any, please have the money wired to the address supplied.*

*I wish I could provide even the slightest sense of the beauty of this world. The photographs won't. It's been the wonder-drug for all my ailments. My kidneys have been on their best behavior. I'm even sleeping!*

*There've been many challenges but they've all been swept away by the joy. I have many new friends. Everywhere the light and air invigorates. Everywhere the smell of the flowers— especially the tiare, a tiny white gardenia that the girls and boys wear in the hair and touch to their lips, and then their pelvis, before handing to you—intoxicates. And the trade winds, the trade winds, all night and all morning, never cease to blow in Tahiti. In this life, one feels there's no work, and no worries; the*

*shining days go by in games and dancing, bathing and fishing,
and the night innocently brings all lovers together.*

*Are you surprised at such a fulsome letter? See how I've
changed!*

*When I think I'll have to leave all of this, I already suffer the
agony of departure. I've been here less than a month and I don't
want to be anywhere else. The thought of Los Angeles or Berlin
is repulsive to me. I want to be alone, or with a few rare people.
When I sit outside my bungalow in the evening and watch the
waves break one by one and thunder on the reef, I feel terribly
small, and wish I were home. But I'm never "at home,"
anywhere. I feel this more and more, the older I get—not in any
country, nor in any house, nor with anyone.*

*I hope you're well. My best to Bernhard and Robert. As for
Father—every day I think of him with sadness. The remorse I
carry around since childhood is that of the landholder's son
who in disobedience to his father's wishes left the estate in alien
hands.*

*But all of this is just to let you know that I'm well, and to
prod you into sending as much news as possible. Warmest
wishes to you, from your most loving*

Willi

By the 25th of July, Flaherty and Murnau were barely speaking. At times David acted as an intermediary, and Flaherty occasionally came round to the veranda and they sat together in morose silence like an old married couple. Flaherty was miserable and angry about the final version of the film's story, but it was Murnau's money, and Murnau's picture.

By that point it had become a simple tale of love in the face of the curse of the *tabu*. As a concession to Flaherty, the story had been set against the contrast between the lovers' paradisical atoll and the "civilized" island of the merchants and missionaries. Murnau, too, saw the latter as a sad place steeped in alcohol and jazz. Flaherty kept insisting that the death of a people was their real subject; that they couldn't turn back the clock. They had to film *what was there.*

Murnau's reply was that Flaherty hadn't worried so much about that in his earlier films. Hadn't he invented activities for his noble primitives in both *Nanook* and *Moana*? Hadn't he in both films taught the natives fishing techniques they'd long ago abandoned?

Murnau's questions, David had later remarked, had been one of the low points in their negotiations.

In the afternoon heat they had the veranda to themselves. The Scots uniformly napped, and the Frenchmen lounged about inside, one to a table. They looked for the most part even more miserable than Flaherty. They weren't interested in sociability; it wasn't what their kind of tropical drinking was all about. Those who couldn't find separate tables dragged chairs up to the wainscoting.

Pal had been overcome with a particularly vicious type of flea and some version of mange. Crosby had cut his thumb and was trying to work with a cartoon bandage. Flaherty was known to prefer more than one drink, and had been drinking heavily. He spent his afternoons sitting around making fun of Murnau's hat. David continually capped his bottle or offered to put it away, which inevitably would initiate a short spat.

With the change of seasons, most days began poorly, with spoiled fruit for breakfast. On final location-checks, the surf often ran high when they returned from their anchorages. Confusion around the tiller would periodically cause their away-boat to broach to. Some production notes would be lost. After one capsizing, Flaherty's pocket watch became a tiny aquarium; for the next few days he showed off a minuscule shrimp traversing the water beneath its face.

The long-awaited first day of shooting was delayed when one of the camera cases was dropped off the dock. Cleaning the camera took the next three days of Crosby's time. The more intimate portions of the mechanism were coated with salt.

Waiting for the camera, they passed days of airless quiet and great heat. Shell-gatherers were warned from the beaches. The highest palms hung motionless, and nothing was audible but the long lines of breakers. The trades were noticeable at the highest elevations only around dusk.

Each day they lunched on parrot fish and rice pudding, squinting out at the intense glare of a cloudless oceanic afternoon. Murnau's bare feet would usually be in the sun and he'd be distracted by the worry that they were already getting pink. As if they had nothing better to do, they resumed their argument.

Flaherty would assert that they had a responsibility to the truth. Murnau would respond, in his schoolmaster's tone, that truth wasn't in the slavish recording of data but in the emotion and the drama. A filmed record of the islands would convey their essence no more effectively than a fictionalized drama. All memories were acts of imagination, and to assume anything else was bottomless innocence.

"I find it completely characteristic that you don't drink," Flaherty stated at one point, apropos of nothing. Neither David nor Murnau responded.

Mr. Drunkard refused to believe that Murnau's abstinence was due to kidney trouble.

The arguments came to nothing. Knowing how fond Murnau was of the *Bali*, Flaherty took to wearing heavy-soled shoes that would scratch the polished deck.

But it was Murnau's job to hold their little group together. He told Flaherty he was sorry they'd gotten to this position, and that Flaherty's film was not lost. There'd still be much of the sort of thing he wanted to record: the hunters' strength and honesty, a

Nature at once bountiful and pitiless, as well as the heartbreak of the slow disintegration of paradise.

But *Tabu* would not pretend that it was not a film. It would make use of the tricks of the trade. They would be done discreetly or not at all. They'd point up the emphasis of the story and not disfigure it.

Flaherty listened impatiently to such talk and then would get up and lurch inside to replace his bottle. Often he wouldn't reappear for half an hour, and his brother would finally go to look for him.

One afternoon after David brought him back, they all watched Mehao spearfishing a hundred yards down the beach. At that distance he had the appearance of a dark Aeneas. His dress was traditional but his spear was metal, probably from San Francisco.

Murnau finally remarked that he didn't think it was possible any longer to get an idea of the old Tahitian customs by observation. It was like staring at a Norwegian and hoping to learn about the Vikings.

Flaherty responded that he'd asked the natives who worked at the Residency about that boy. They'd described him as a *mahu*. An effeminate person.

The comment had no effect on Murnau. He took a sip of his lime drink. He gazed at Flaherty, and Flaherty gazed back. Finally, Murnau told Flaherty that he would make this as clear as he could. He was finished arguing with him: Flaherty was now a hired hand.


THE SHOOTING, when it did begin, went poorly. Mehao was a distraction to everyone as Murnau's assistant.

.  .  .

ON THE second day, Flaherty remarked to the group that the Polynesians were subject to diseases of the will as well as the body. They had a word for it: *erimatua*. It wasn't in Murnau's dictionary. Those who contracted it literally died of discouragement. This was accepted as unavoidable by the victim's family.

SADNESS AND guilt became the gently insistent theme of Murnau's time with Mehao. They flared up like cold on a damaged tooth.

Mehao noticed. He had a sweet and gentle nature and an acumen for business that was startling. He was an inveterate flirt. He was married. When Murnau asked about his wife, on Fatuhiva, Mehao said, *"Aita pea-pea"*: it doesn't matter.

In the small of his back he had two indentations, like the press of thumbs.

The morning after the decisive argument with Flaherty, they woke around three. The air was scented. Murnau was on his side, his cheek on Mehao's hand. Off the veranda, a half-moon lit the surf along the shore. A black crane fished in the swirling water, stepping brokenly about.

By five Mehao was gone. Just after sunrise, Murnau flung himself into the smooth warm water of the lagoon. He anchored on his seat a few yards offshore in the soft sand, his face to the morning sun low across the water. Afterwards he took a shower bath and moved to his veranda chair for coffee and warm rolls with honey.

Flaherty emerged from his room looking hungover. He fetched his own coffee from the kitchen and returned, propping his ankles on the veranda rail alongside Murnau, as though they were two Bavarians on the Spree. He looked at Murnau with the poker-playing expression of someone who'd experienced a catastrophic setback and fancied it didn't show on his face. He said,

"Well, whatever the virtues of the Tahitian, chasteness is not one of them."

A SHORT letter from Murnau's mother came in the morning mail packet. It made no mention of his letter. Apparently she'd just seen *Tartüff* at her local theater. She wrote, "The silver and china are always so exquisite in your films." He pinned up the letter next to his looking glass.

The looking glass hung on a string and trembled when the trades were blowing. His red hair, his wrinkles, his age, his freckles: every morning there was the altogether draining surprise of his own coarseness.

By the 14th of August he'd received reports from four island groups, but not a single word about Spiess.

David spent much of his time placating the local "chief." They paid for "protection," as if in Chicago. Only by promising so much a week could they insure cooperation and prevent "fishing fleets" from crossing back and forth behind their shots.

Crosby meanwhile spent days on a tramline for the dolly. Constructing one on uneven ground caused him no end of aggravation. He carried everywhere his little notebook and *The Carpenters' and Builders' Manual*. His constant fear that he'd overlooked something important gave him a restless aspect.

Once he built the thing, all night the native girls and boys rolled his cart up and down its tracks. No one was able to sleep. Then the great joke became to derail the cart over and over. This they thought irresistably funny. Crosby, Flaherty, and Murnau finally went out to put a stop to the proceedings, and became part of the hilarity. Finally the revelers were shooed away, and Crosby stood guard over the dolly cart until morning.

The shots that they got with the dolly over the next week proved unusable.

. . .

BY MID-AUGUST, Pal seemed reinvigorated. At any given moment during a discussion they would notice him in the background against the tall grass and the skyline, flying through the air after birds. The islanders called him the Bouncing Dog.

AROUND THE veranda were innumerable crab holes, from which big land crabs emerged to work their way over to leaves or fallen blossoms. They ate anything. One pulled the end of Murnau's towel down its hole.

EVERY SO often they had a good night, when, thanks to a few moments with the actors or the light, Murnau had the impression that the day had gone well, and that it was all right for work to have ended.

On nights like that he set up magnesium torches around the lagoon for midnight swims with Mehao. Crosby was furious at the waste. But when they dived from the tall rocks and sprayed white light high into the air, they were like magically shining ghosts in the otherwise black water. Other Tahitians joined them, naked. Their wet bodies shimmered in the torchlight. The women held palm leaf fans before their faces.

****24 AUGUST. Every position is unposed and singular; he possesses his body as others possess music. He's the jungle in person, though his cheekbones and black eyes are those of a Breton peasant.

Eroticism is the true subject of film. Asta Nielsen, and the way she suggested nudity with only her eyes.

Film brings the overintellectualized back into the primal realm of gesture, and allows us to recover the breathtaking power of primal communication. It lets us breathe, not speak. The new world I seek here is not a world of novelty and wonder but *intuition*.

Since Nature's so generously inclined toward them, these people must create their own tragedies. So they have their tradition in which the eldest choose maidens as priestesses for the gods— maidens who then may no longer love men. They become "tabu."

Mehao uses my sense of his exoticism as a screen. Which is more blinding to the truth: the fetishism of the colonialist or the mimicry of the native?

****LIGHTNING all night. An ominous reminder of the fever curve. Toward morning, a promising little breeze. Around breakfast, an attack of flies.

****26 AUGUST.　Crosby and Flaherty asked me to walk the beach with them. Discipline was breaking down, they reported. The project was coming apart. Changes had to be made. The shooting schedule had to be tightened. Unessential personnel had to be released. Crosby cited the uncertain weather not far off.

I told them I thought things were going well. Some listless haggling followed. At one point I sat in the waves' wrack at the edge of a tidal pool. As the rushing water withdrew, marvels of color and design streamed through my fingers. I caught only the occasional conch or miracle spiral as proof of what I'd missed with each wave's retreat.

At lunch they tried again. The orange of Tahiti is delicious: small and sweet with a thin, dry rind. Mehao visible from the veranda, spearfishing again. The palm-tree tattoo accentuated the muscles in his back. A minor and sad surprise: he's spent some of the money I gave him on a straw boater's hat. The bickering with Crosby and F. petered out.

At dusk we set up Crosby's camera at the edge of the break-water reef for some sunset shots. In places, we were walking on the roof of immense subterranean caverns. The sea rushed into them with uncanny noise, geysering mist and spray through the cracks. It made me feel fifteen years old.

Flaherty took the occasion to deliver a lesson on the local folk-lore. There was throughout Tahitian culture an element of dread. Fears of demons and the dark were deeply written in the Polyne-sian mind. Presences called *vehinehae* made the nocturnal road-side, and particularly the crossroads, frightful; they were like mist shaped as men and with the eyes of cats. They represented the dead. When a native said he was a man, he meant a man and not a demon, instead of a man and not a beast. Only recently, after twi-light, Flaherty said, a demon was said to have taken the younger of two boys to the edge of the jungle. The demon was said to have whispered "You are so-and-so, son of so-and-so?" and then caressed and beguiled the boy deeper into the undergrowth while his older brother watched, petrified.

We all stood about while his little parable was supposed to be sinking in. He added that the natives believed white blood to be talismanic against the powers of hell. It was the only way that they could explain the unpunished recklessness of the Europeans.

I made no comment. Finally, Flaherty blurted out, "They're dying, for God's sake! The main thing is to let them die in peace."


****30 AUGUST.    Received a card from Wagner in Berlin. He is well. Max Schreck is going to star as General von Seeckt in a play called *Poison Gas Over Berlin.* Apparently based on a real inci-dent, hushed up, involving a medium bomber that almost crashed the previous summer in the Tiergarten. Sure to raise a hullabaloo about the rearmament policies. Reminds me of the furor surrounding a Toller play at the Grosses Schauspielhaus about an infernal machine that stood for something pernicious in German society (authority? bureaucracy? beer?). The play was always being shut down in the second act by a storm of applause, or of whistling, seat-pounding, and catcalls.

****2 SEPTEMBER. Finally: Spiess.

An envelope addressed to me was discovered at the Residency on an island due north of here, Starbuck Island. Inside was a latitude and longitude. I left that day, with Crosby.

It was a two-day sail to a place called Phoenix Island. On the second afternoon it emerged from a blue haze, the culmination of all this searching. Then the clouds rolled in and took it away.

At the pier we asked about Europeans. No one knew anything. Crosby suggested using francs, and it quickly became evident how many francs were involved. Crosby reminded me that the amount further damaged our already chaotic budget.

We were led through the jungle, streaming sweat. The heat was otherworldly. We dream-walked through the vegetation in a covered house of heat. The air was breathless, though overhead the river of trade winds streamed without pause.

Finally we came to the wreck of a hut, surrounded by high weeds. Behind the hut was a long, cleared field. On the field: Aviatiks!

Three old two-seaters, two with cannibalized engines. All three had long since lost their fabric.

War relics, it was explained.

I stood among them, speechless. Allmenröder's face came back to me. I'd heard of aircraft shipped around the world to protect German interests.

"Did you fly in these?" Crosby asked.

Our guide demanded payment. Crosby took him aside.

An oilskin packet was lashed to the stick in the first plane's forward cockpit. On it someone had drawn one of Grau's old cabalistic signs from *Nosferatu*. The letter inside read:

*My Inhibited Murnau, if you get this far—*

*Remember these? I thought it would be salutary for you to view them again.*

*Received word from associates in Papeete that your confederate has arrived and that you're on your way. So I'm on my way as well. We have our boat, and we're off: The Solomons, New Guinea, Indonesia, Japan, San Francisco, our fortune. My friends do not wish to meet you. I do not wish for you to meet them.*

*I promise the cessation of all packages. I wish us both peace of mind, whatever we did. We were young. We were fools: all three of us. We've done our penance.*

*What our friend did or didn't do is his affair. No?*

*It's his affair.*

*I wish you good luck on your project. I wish you long life—*

*Your friend Hecate.*

It was dated 1 July: just about the time we arrived.

OUR GUIDE offered to sell us the Aviatiks.

MURNAU'S RELATIONSHIP with Flaherty ended in mid-September. David grew increasingly despondent about their quarrels and took to drinking as much as his brother. Some evenings he was confined to his chair by inebriation. During one of those nights, he let slip a story from Flaherty's filming of *Moana* in Samoa, in 1923.

Flaherty had become good friends with a German trader. The trader had done a great deal to facilitate their welcome with the natives. After two of Flaherty's lab-assistants killed another native in a dispute, the trader and Flaherty had a falling-out, the former accusing him of obstructing the course of justice by refusing to hand the two over to the authorities. Flaherty, however, was determined not to lose weeks training new lab-assistants. He leveled countercharges against both the Resident Commissioner, who'd taken the trader's side, and the trader himself, claiming they were homosexuals who'd preyed upon Samoans. The Commissioner was told that the charges would be dropped if he left the country. He committed suicide that night. The trader, after being arrested, tried, and banished, committed suicide on the steamer carrying him back to Europe.

Even drunk, David had been unable to look at Murnau throughout the recounting of the story.

The next morning, Murnau terminated his partnership with Flaherty. It was arranged that Flaherty would buy out his share for five thousand dollars, to be paid when he next had five thousand dollars. Both Flahertys, it was decided, would leave by mail steamer for San Francisco within the next two weeks.

Crosby meanwhile came down with a case of blood poisoning.

IN OCTOBER, Murnau received from Else Lasker-Schüler a short and heartbroken letter that had taken over two years to find him. Paul had died of tuberculosis in Berlin. At the point of death he had requested that she step behind the bed curtain so that he could die alone. Lasker-Schüler's handwriting had deteriorated so badly in the attempt to write the letter that it took Murnau countless rereadings to extract some of the details. She was, she said, making an effort to recover some of what she'd cherished, and was making lists in her letters to friends. He'd collected clocks, and had scrutinized the workings of the little wheels for hours, the way a machinist watched his contraptions. When still in his high chair, he had sketched a blackbird and had said, "I've drawn a crow that steals meat." His favorite word had been *Persia*. His favorite breakfast had been an egg beaten with sugar. Of his sketch pads, Karl Arnold had once said, "He doesn't draw; he swims across the paper." However bitterly she and he had argued, they'd always known that they'd be sitting beside each other that evening at the movies.

MURNAU SPENT the whole next day trying to compose a telegram. All he could conjure up were Paul's sad eyes. And then his mother, distracted and anxious, jingling her jewelry in somebody's face. When he once had voiced impatience with both of them, Hans had answered, "Is it really so hard, every so often, to sustain a thought for somebody else?"

THE FLAHERTYS left without saying goodbye. Crosby kept to himself, disappearing for days at a stretch. Murnau found himself with energy for neither work nor Mehao, who accepted his impassiveness and simply sat in the room with him, hands together on his thighs. He seemed to recognize that they were grieving. *"Kare-peka,"* he said. It's all right.

ANOTHER BOY took to following them around. He was thirteen years old and told Murnau through hand signs that he wished to see his ship.

IN NOVEMBER, Mehao finally became concerned enough to lead Murnau into the jungle late one night. He made clear that he wanted to show him something.

For a while they kept to a road of crushed coral. Pal came along, trotting beside them.

They passed villages spotted with yellow light. Those who'd recently lost relations kept kerosene lamps burning to turn the spirits away. Now and then bicycle riders passed them, indistinct ghosts with tinkling bells.

They left the road for a grassy track. The canopy overhead prevented even starlight from providing illumination. It was so dark that Murnau was without opinions. He was completely in Mehao's hands. Unknown things brushed and swept against him.

On an island so mountainous, the only means of penetrating the interior was to work one's way up the valleys. The valleys began to narrow, the sides growing precipitous. He and Mehao climbed for hours, while the ravine narrowed to the width of a streambed. The sides were vertical, with vegetation choking every handhold. Pal labored over obstacles, scrabbling on the loose debris in the dark.

The ravine finally opened into a narrow track spanning a ridge, far above the tree canopy.

The sky began to pale. The track led to a large flat rock above a precipice six hundred feet high. The abyss was partially concealed by overhanging ferns and lilies. The Alps have a grander scale, Murnau thought, but for abruptness of the fall, nothing compared with this.


THERE MEHAO extracted his gift from his shirt: a small folded parcel of leaves containing starfruit and two unripe bananas. A picnic, intended to cheer up his friend.

Murnau thanked him. The boy made them comfortable in a hollowed-out notch in the rock a foot or so back from the edge. Then he pointed out an interesting feature of the track off to the east, where it bordered an innocent-looking bank of moderate steepness. He was pointing to a notorious spot about which Murnau had been warned. The bank grew steeper in the center, where the slope was nearly 65 degrees. Off the track the grass was cropped short by the goats, and slippery. There was nothing on which to catch hold, and every so often a hiker would slip. He could slow himself, but not stop. His slide proceeded from exasperating to terrifying, and from there off into space. The place was called the Judgment Seat. The boy didn't know why.

The two of them contemplated the slippery grass without speaking. Beyond it they could see the Residency. The light was brightening behind the islands to the east. The mountain ranges were lifting into relief. Attenuated clouds took flight overhead.

He began to weep. He took the boy's hand. Who knew what he'd left untouched and what he'd polluted? Who knew what he had yet to ruin? The boy lifted their clasped hands and brought them to his chest. Again he seemed content to sit and respect his friend's incomprehensible grieving.

It was as if freedom were an endless, snowy plain. He had come to make a movie. He had conceived the idea, sold it, talked his collaborators into working with him, raised a crew, sailed to the islands, written the story, and dealt with the collapse of funding. He had overseen the casting, the locations, the schedule, and the natives' training and discipline. He'd ferried groups about, fought, ordered, wheedled, lied, seduced, abandoned, settled disputes, hated, and loved. He'd attempted to snatch opportunity as it had revealed itself.

Crosby had been wonderful throughout. Half the time he'd had no tripod, his thin body trying to hold the top-heavy Akeley steady while Murnau directed over his shoulder. One day they'd gotten thirty shots in four hours, in a boat, on a pitching sea, with native actors, and broken cloud cover changing the light every two minutes. Crosby had been the hero of the expedition.

Murnau had told him, before the final falling-out with the Flahertys, that he thought Crosby's name should go first in the credit titles. Crosby had answered that he thought *Tabu* should have special *dis*credit titles: *"This Film Was Made in* Spite *of—..."*

THE FORGOTTEN Pal was whining a ledge below because he couldn't reach them. "I'm here," Murnau called quietly to him. "I'm here," he called again, this time in German.

What his art lacked, he knew, was passionate humanity. His love for the world was distant and severe. Three-quarters of his life had had nothing to do with what he'd accomplished professionally.

Even now he was with someone while being almost completely elsewhere. He was a boy, happy to run errands, buy bread, butter, greens, and his father's tobacco. He was consulting his errand-list. He was carrying two kilos of weisswurst. He was holding his future before him, a magic box with a lethal surprise.

His father was talking. He was speaking to his son Wilhelm, and young Wilhelm studied his voice and reminded himself to value the lessons being offered. In the street outside, his brothers tossed balls and shouted. They splashed through the runoff after the rain.

Where was it his father was shouting from, telling him to bring the hose and do some watering, with everything so dry? Someone was crying. Someone had climbed the tree to pick a basket of cherries. Wilhelm ran over with the hose on his shoulder, but couldn't find his father. In the garden in the heat, something was twittering. The breeze made small dust devils on the patio.

FOR THE fourteen years since Hans's death Murnau had betrayed him. He had betrayed himself by pretending he hadn't. He had cherished his feelings for Hans as something sacred and untouchable and had worked to replicate them in a nearly endless stream of substitutes. He was a man of austere principles without principles. He was a man committed only to a personal art whose inner life never saw the light of day. When he considered the phases of who he had been, every step forward might just as well have been a retreat, and the line he traced of his own silhouette was ever more cloaked. Publicly he had lived a deception. Privately, too. To try to remember where he'd entered the shadows, or where the shadows had entered him, was pointless. The shadows had been there from the beginning.

Before the boy had come to get him that night, he had made another attempt to revise the ending of the film. He had written a rough version of the farewell note the woman would leave for her lover before being taken away for good to satisfy the *tabu*.

*I have been*
*so happy with you.*
*Far more than I deserved.*
*The love you have*
*given me*
*I will keep*
*to the last beat*
*of my heart.*
*Across the great waters*
*I will come to you*
*when the moon*
*spreads its fate*
*on the sea.*
*Farewell.*

He was shoulder to shoulder with this Polynesian boy. The boy's smell was on his lips. The sun was a few degrees above an orange horizon. The final image of the film was already set in his mind, a shot on which he'd decided months ago: the image of the *tabu* woman's lover, a lone swimmer in pursuit of her boat, swimming until he drowned.

The sun rose above them. Mehao leaned his dark head back and listened, taking pleasure in his friend's inscrutable sounds. Murnau talked to his father in German, and to Pal in English. He apologized to Mehao. He apologized to Hans. He recited aloud from memory from de Bougainville's journals, on the discovery of Polynesia: *"We found companies of men sitting in the shade of their fruit trees. They greeted us with signs of friendship. Those who met us on the road stood aside to let us pass by. And everywhere we found hospitality, ease, innocent joy, and every appearance of happiness amongst them."*

# RIGA,
# 1915

7. July 1915
Somewhere in Lettland

My Dear Murnau,

Your last letter hurtled me out of a clear blue sky and into a rain cloud—or something very like one. My apologies for the delay in answering. I'm pleased you liked your packet of gifts. Lately I've been taking pleasure in being a poor correspondent, something I might indulge in completely were I a pure artist, which is to say, an eccentric. What a prospect!

We lie here on the riverbank, the location a military secret, and to the south all is forest and marshland. There are swarms of gnats.

I meant to write you yesterday, but today is hazy and dreary, and the glory of inspiration is long past.

I'll try to apply myself to some of your many questions. Mother's fine, though reading between the lines I can see that she's having her heart difficulties again. I've heard from various members of the New Youth; they sent along a review praising some tense "futuristic" lyrics by various dirty little boys, and sneering at my naïve stuff.

I've recovered only slowly from the news about Marc. I've written his poor wife. He was in vintage form in his last letter, declaiming that our ideals would in the future have to be fed on "grasshoppers and wild honey, and not on history." I assume he's closer now to those Secret Forces in the universe.

As for my risk-taking, on my worst days it's a form of cynical recklessness. Every so often I give way to an intrepid madness and do things that garner praise. I've been put up for a decoration.

Did I once dislike the Russians? Briefly. November or December of last year.

And I disagree, again: Achilles does seem to me the greatest of all the Greeks, not only for his martial supremacy but because of the intensity of his love for his companion. Nothing in him seems nobler than the despair which makes him despise life once he's lost his beloved. As Lasker-S—— once said: When love has gone out of someone's life, the heart engulfs the head.

Occasionally I think about my own safety. I wonder: What does this chaos hold in store for me. A field hospital? Will I be crippled? Lose my hand? Lose my sight!

And what about you, broken-down friend? Bad back, bad headaches, bad stomach. A deck chair really should be made ready for you somewhere in a garden back in Berlin, half in the shade, with ten glasses of milk within easy reach. Is this impossible? Is there no one to make it possible? What does your doctor say?

I've often thought that life for you is something entirely different than it is for the rest of us. Everything's all or nothing with you. Everything's very puzzling and absorbing, the way a locomotive is for a small child. The whole world is something you hold in high regard, because it's good at what it does.

The photo you sent is not reassuring. That pale, drawn visage, those fixed eyes and tall body held straight by force of will all suggest Pluto, God of Shades. Or the Thracian Horseman, that mysterious figure seen riding through the copses by moonlight, carrying away the souls of the dead in the folds of his cloak.

I understand your despair over your father's letter. You can't read anything new into it; I wouldn't try. It's cordial and heartfelt and brutish, and in my opinion, your only answer can be what someone who loves you would say to him on your behalf: *Leave this man alone. He's attempting to live the way he should. He's not asking for "accommodation." He's only asking for you to speak with him as one human to another, and not close yourself off to him in a fury. This is the only power you have to diminish the sorrow in both your lives.*

Do your remember our trip to Zwickau? Do you remember the fire lilies and purple gentians? Do you remember that black dog in the snow, on the way to your namesake town? The strong red tea, with our English breakfast?

The unit's all up and about. We'll be tramping somewhere soon. I have questions for you, as well. How's our friend Lubitsch, and what does he think—should we declare war on America or not? Have you heard any more about Lasker-S—— and Twardowski? What about Paul?

If I survive this spastic war, the summit of an unreal, unspiritual time, I want out of civilized Europe. I want to collect my strength for action elsewhere. I want to join others in acting and not remain dreaming and sleeping. I want to be allowed to be myself without lies, without masks. I want all this before life is snatched away, leaving the ideal image, which disappears, of the bravest swimmer drowning.

I have no idea how I'll strike you when I finally return from here, all battered and burned out. I'm at work every day at mastering my emotions. Soon I'll be atop the situation. I wish you all good fortune. Hand in hand with you, I wish you quiet nights, a quiescent front, and many packages from home.

Warmest wishes to you. Remember my prediction—

Hans

7. July 1915
A trench—Riga.

Hans, Hans, Hans,

Still no rest for your sleepless friend. Wildflowers are blooming all around. The fields are filled with a hay that no one cuts and no one uses, other than our "field gray," to make temporary camps on the damp ground. A warm wind blows clouds and rain over us, and the nights are a complete darkness that one believes could be grabbed in the hand. I'm living in a dugout that reminds me of the heatherhut in *Lear:* much straw and rain, a lantern and a little madness; only the Fool is missing. I'm so endlessly alone that it's almost pleasant. Unfortunately there's always the constraint that stands behind the loneliness. The fact that I can't suddenly change my situation inhibits the pleasure.

I've separated myself from the criminal mindlessness that's the rule here, so there's an obliviousness to me among my compatriots that's breathtaking. Unless I actively seek out a group and insert myself into it—always unbidden, and usually unacknowledged—I spend my time alone. I'm approached only when it's time for memorials or eulogies. I'm also the accepted authority on cultural activities.

I've become the unofficial quartermaster, due to my perceived fussiness. Schedules, shipments, complaints, aggravations, detritus—my head's a railroad station. Every so often the Captain rings up and I'm called on the carpet, the whole swindle about to come out. At such times I should be visualized like that boy we saw in the garden in Königsplatz, staring into space like an idiot.

With all our recent movements, the regular mail has not arrived. It's doubtful that anything will come tomorrow, either. The day before yesterday we were in a village that brought me closer to you geographically than any time since Friedrichstadt.

Are you still dug in? Are you safe behind your fortifications? A view of your escarpment, please.

Müthel recently passed through, with his unit. They were headed east! We had a short conversation on politics. He certainly is one of his family; you'd think you were listening to the father, with a little more humor. Still, he's a good fellow, a Marc-type, not conventional, with eyes and a heart.

Speaking of that, more ugly news: Veidt wrote that a friend of his was beaten to death in a hotel catering to sailors in Hamburg. Twenty-two years old. The news made me contemplate again how few fulfill themselves before death. I resolved to judge all interrupted careers with more pity.

It's been so long since we conversed. What will happen when you see me? The door will open and an emaciated beanstalk will be swaying there, finally smiling (incessantly, and more out of embarrassment than pleasure). He'll then sit where he's told. When the welcoming ceremonies are over, he'll scarcely speak, since he lacks the strength to do so. And he won't even be as happy as he feels he should be, lacking the strength even for that.

Hans! What you are for me can't be found in the scraps I send you. Remember when you argued for the writer's greater pleasure, for moving others across time and space? How did people ever get the idea that they could communicate adequately by letter—?

You complain about my letters that there "isn't a single word that isn't well-weighed." And yet those are the letters by which I hope to draw myself closer to you.

I can no longer lament the falling-apart. I lament instead the wait for the rebuilding.

But listen to me: I should be making clear that I'm only frightened and self-berating. Instead I posture. I pose.

Throughout our time together I have forced you to settle for murmured sounds and inattentive ears. Forgive me.

I don't know how to approach my other subject. I begin by saying that about my own fidelity I deceived myself, the way a teacher, out of exhaustion and yearning, allows himself to be convinced that one correct answer means that his student now comprehends the subject.

Be patient. Your letters are rain on my forehead. My letters are words spoken into your ear while you lie beside me, turning toward my mouth.

Do you know when you were most beautifully dressed, on that trip to Murnau? There can't be any argument about it: the night we arrived.

I want to go back to that moment.

I realize that I deserve to be hit in the face for speaking beyond *this* moment, which belongs to you.

When I was a child, I did something very bad, though not in the public sense but only in my private reckoning. (The fact that it wasn't publicly acknowledged as bad confirmed my suspicion that the adult world was asleep.) Afterwards, I was amazed that nothing had changed: the grown-ups, though somewhat gloomy, had gone about their business, their mouths shut in the natural way I'd admired from below since my earliest days.

What I'm most frightened of is experiencing the eclipse of love: seeing those eyes that were home to me close themselves off forever.

What will happen to me? Even if I sit among people until my last breath, welcomed, embraced, and initiated into their secrets, I'll never be one of them.

What I wrote to do was to ask forgiveness. Instead, with your image before me, I return to my own solitude.

Many greetings to your mother. I send you all that I'm unable to say to you. I wish you God's safety. Write. Write to your Murnau. I wish I could say more—

ON MARCH 10, 1931, with his own car in the shop, Murnau rented a light blue Packard for a two-day drive from Los Angeles to Monterey. Twelve miles south of Santa Barbara, his chauffeur stopped for gas at the Rio Grande Oil Station. When the chauffeur returned to the car, Murnau's house-servant, a young Filipino, was seated at the wheel.

The Filipino told the chauffeur that Murnau had said he could drive. Murnau, seated in the back seat with Pal, didn't confirm or deny the claim.

The Filipino drove for approximately five miles. The chauffeur records having protested repeatedly that he was driving too fast.

At about that time, Murnau is supposed to have said from the back seat, "Pal is frightened." These were his last recorded words.

At six-thirty or so the Packard slung itself sideways off a bend and rolled over once. At first all of its occupants, including Pal, seemed unhurt. Murnau was found twenty feet from the car, conscious but unable, or unwilling, to speak. He was admitted to the Santa Barbara College Hospital. He died the following morning, fifteen years and two hundred and twenty-six days after the death of his friend Hans.

ACKNOWLEDGMENTS

This novel is a work of imagination. That imagination would have been pitifully undernourished without the contributions of the following texts:

Gerd Albrecht and Klaus Becker's *Friedrich Wilhelm Murnau: Ein Grosser Filmregisseur der 20er Jahre;* Uta Berg-Ganschow and Wolfgang Jacobsen's *Film . . . Stadt . . . Kino . . . Berlin;* Janet Bergstrom's "Sexuality at a Loss: The Films of F. W. Murnau"; Luciano Berriatua's *Los Proverbios Chinos de F. W. Murnau;* Hans-Michael Bock and Wolfgang Jacobsen's *Film-Materialien: Henrik Galeen;* Robert Bresson's *Notes on Cinematography;* Karl Brown's *Adventures with D. W. Griffith;* Jean Cocteau's *Diary of a Film;* Alan Clark's *Aces High;* Richard Dyer's "Children of the Night"; Lotte Eisner's *Murnau* and *The Haunted Screen;* David Flaherty's "A Few Reminiscences"; Lewis Freeman's *In the Tracks of the Trades;* Karl Freund's "Die Berufung des Kameramannes"; Peter Fritzsche's *A Nation of Fliers: German Aviation and the Popular Imagination;* Ken Gelder's *Reading the Vampire;* Johann Wolfgang von Goethe's *Conversations with Eckermann;* Albin Grau's "Licht-Regie im Film"; Richard Griffith's *The World of Robert Flaherty;* Ursula Hardt's *Erich Pommer: Film Producer for Germany;* Charles W. Haxthausen and Heidrun Suhr's *Berlin: Culture and Metropolis;* Robert Herlth and

Walter Röhrig's "Der Dämon im Glashaus: Eine Skizze von Arbeit am Faust-Film"; Ernst Hofmann's *Aus Briefen F. W. Murnaus: Der Mensch und der Kunstler;* Christopher Isherwood's *Christopher and His Kind, Prater Violet,* and *Lions and Shadows;* Franz Kafka's *Letters to Milena;* Klaus Kreimeier's *The Ufa Story;* Else Lasker-Schüler's *Concert;* Hector MacQuarrie's *Tahiti Days;* Roland Marz and Rosemarie Radeke's *Von der Dada-Messe zum Bildersturm DIX + Berlin;* Victor Meisel's *Voices of German Expressionism;* John H. Morrow, Jr.,'s *German Air Power in World War I;* Robert Newton's *Your Diamond Dreams Cut Open My Arteries: Poems by Else Lasker-Schüler;* Aaron Norman's *The Great Air War;* Frederick O'Brien's *Mystic Isles of the South Seas;* Graham Petrie's *Hollywood Destinies;* Michael Powell's *Edge of the World;* Eberhard Roters's *Berlin 1910–1933;* Rainer Rother's *Ufa-Magazine NR. 5: Faust,* from *Die Ufa 1917–1945: Das Deutsche Bildimperium;* Thomas J. Saunders's *Hollywood in Berlin;* Oliver Sayler's *Max Reinhardt and His Theatre; The Letters and Diaries of Oskar Schlemmer* (Tut Schlemmer, ed.); Eberhard Spiess's *Wenn Ihr Affen nur ofter schreiben wolltet!: Briefwechsel zwischen Friedrich Wilhelm Murnau und Lothar Müthel;* Robert Louis Stevenson's *In the South Seas;* Walter Thielemann's "Nosferatu: Der Neue Weg im Film"; Paul Virilio's *War and Cinema;* Thomas Waugh's "Murnau: The Films Behind the Man"; and Robin Wood's "The Dark Mirror: Murnau's *Nosferatu.*"

I'M ALSO grateful for the assistance of the following institutions: the Armchair Sailor Bookstore, in Newport, Rhode Island; the Deutsche Bundesarchiv-Militararchiv, in Freiburg; the Deutsches Institut für Filmkunde, in Frankfurt; the Goethe-Institut, in New York; the Krankenbuchlager, Berlin; the Staatliches Filmarchiv, Berlin; the Stiftung Deutsche Kinemathek, Berlin; and Williams College.

· · ·

I THANK the following individuals, for their time, their support, and their particular contributions: Hans Albrecht, Ann Blume, Amy Bottke, Kristin Carter-Sanborn, Gary Fisketjon, Charles Fuqua, Katrin Herzog, Frau Hoffmann, Meredith Hoppin, Thomas Kohut, Peter Matson, Elizabeth Pennebaker, Eberhard Spiess, Werner Sudendorf, and Gary Zebrun.

AND FINALLY, my thanks to two people who can't be thanked enough: Ron Hansen and Karen Shepard. Against all odds, they remained unflagging, optimistic, patient, and rigorous with their editorial advice.

A NOTE ON THE TYPE

THIS BOOK was set in Monotype Dante, a typeface designed by Giovanni Mardersteig (1892–1977). Conceived as a private type for the Officina Bodoni in Verona, Italy, Dante was originally cut only for hand composition by Charles Malin, the famous Parisian punch cutter, between 1946 and 1952. Its first use was in an edition of Boccaccio's *Trattatello in Laude di Dante* that appeared in 1954. The Monotype Corporation's version of Dante followed in 1957. Although modeled on the Aldine type used for Pietro Cardinal Bembo's treatise *De Aetna* in 1495, Dante is a thoroughly modern interpretation of the venerable face.

Composed, printed, and bound by Haddon Craftsmen,
an R. R. Donnelley & Sons Company,
Bloomsburg, Pennsylvania
Designed by Virginia Tan